...wing hot air)

"...The humorous writing, wacky names, lively, cartoonlike illustrations, and simple text will especially appeal to reluctant readers."

—*Kirkus Reviews*

"This is a happily silly introduction to the world of fantasy and tabletop gaming, and Fart is sure to fight his way into readers' hearts, especially with the promise of plenty more adventures."

—*The Bulletin of the Center for Children's Books*

"A masterfully crafted love letter to humor and fantasy where every day is a quest to find acceptance, understanding, and friendship. I sincerely look forward to future installments with relish."

—Nick Bruel, creator of the Bad Kitty series

"The story underneath the farts and fun is a great underdog tale about unlikely heroes who discover and celebrate each one's strengths as they learn to trust each other through compassion and sympathy."

—Natalie Watts, school librarian at Huebner Elementary School in San Antonio, Texas

"This book is a superheroic achievement by Aaron Reynolds! At the heart of this book is masterful storytelling with charming characters and a dynamic plot. The humor will keep the readers on their toes, but the adventure will keep them engaged."

—Melissa Lightle, media specialist at Fire Ridge Elementary in Elkhorn, Nebraska

"*Fart Quest* is a laugh-out-loud story of bravery, personal growth, and friendship."

—Laurie Taylor, teacher-librarian at Lakewood Elementary in Tomball, Texas

SQUARE
FISH

An imprint of Macmillan Publishing Group, LLC
120 Broadway, New York, NY 10271 • mackids.com

Square Fish and the Square Fish logo are trademarks of Macmillan and
are used by Roaring Brook Press under license from Macmillan.

Our books may be purchased in bulk for promotional, educational, or
business use. Please contact your local bookseller or the Macmillan
Corporate and Premium Sales Department at (800) 221-7945 ext. 5442
or by email at MacmillanSpecialMarkets@macmillan.com.

Library of Congress Control Number: 2019948766

Originally published in the United States by Roaring Brook Press
First Square Fish edition, 2022
Series design by Cassie Gonzalez
Square Fish logo designed by Filomena Tuosto
Printed in the United States by Lakeside Book Company,
Harrisonburg, Virginia

ISBN 978-1-250-85408-7 (paperback)
1 3 5 7 9 10 8 6 4 2

AR: 3.5

To the silent but deadly Connie Hsu
The Wisdom of a monk
The Strength of a warrior
The Intelligence of a mage
This quest would never have started without you

And

To Steve, Susi, Damian, Jake, and Steph
Mighty Heroes All

Other books in the FART QUEST series

Fart Quest: The Barf of the Bedazzler

Fart Quest: The Dragon's Dookie

AARON REYNOLDS

Illustrated by Cam Kendell

SQUARE
FISH

Roaring Brook Press
New York

DWARVENFORGE

1

THE BRAMBLESHIRE

3

KARBUNKLE
EXPANSE

2

CENTRAL FEY

4

1

14

2

3

5

4

6

7

8

9

ISLE OF MOLAG

5

BLACKROOK
REACH

7

ELVEN KINGDOM
OF KIRAJOY

6

CHAPTER ONE

My name is Fart.

Of course, that's not my real name.

My real name is Bartok. Someday I plan on going by "BARTOK THE BRILLIANT"!

Only try telling that to my master.

"Fart! Take my spellbook! Hurry up and be quick about it!"

That's Elmore the Impressive. He's a mage. A wizard. A sorcerer. A warlock.

Don't know what a mage is?

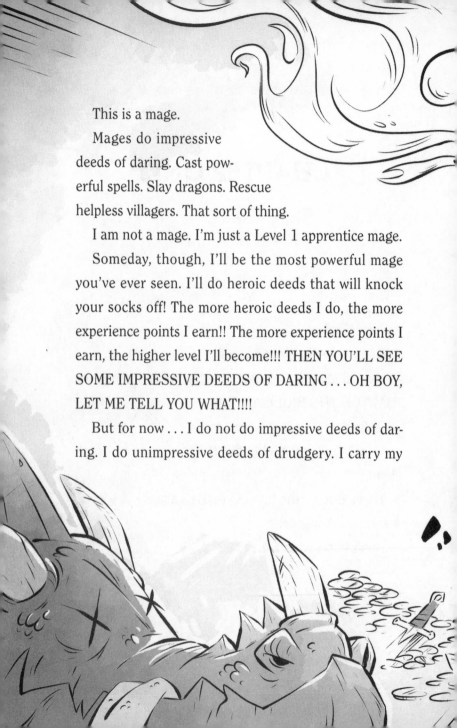

This is a mage.

Mages do impressive deeds of daring. Cast powerful spells. Slay dragons. Rescue helpless villagers. That sort of thing.

I am not a mage. I'm just a Level 1 apprentice mage.

Someday, though, I'll be the most powerful mage you've ever seen. I'll do heroic deeds that will knock your socks off! The more heroic deeds I do, the more experience points I earn!! The more experience points I earn, the higher level I'll become!!! THEN YOU'LL SEE SOME IMPRESSIVE DEEDS OF DARING . . . OH BOY, LET ME TELL YOU WHAT!!!!

But for now . . . I do not do impressive deeds of daring. I do unimpressive deeds of drudgery. I carry my master's impressive spellbook. I iron my master's impressive robes. I wash my master's impressive dishes.

Elmore the Impressive

Impressive pointy hat. (So pointy!)

Impressive fireballs shooting from fingertips. (So fiery!)

Impressive robes. (So soft!)

Impressive spellbook. (So thick!)

There was a time when Elmore the Impressive used to call me Bartok. Not Fart. But that all changed on my spell-picking day, the day a young mage picks his first spell and can actually *use* magic. It's kind of a big deal.

On my spell-picking day, Master Elmore opened his enormous spellbook to page one. "Today is your spell-picking day, boy! You can tell much about the mage an apprentice will become by the first spell they choose."

He held the book out to me. "Look carefully. Consider well. And then choose any first-level spell on the page."

I looked carefully. I considered well.

I could have chosen Magic Missile, which makes a blazing arrow shoot from your fingertips. Super cool.

I could have chosen Frozen Cone, a fun incantation that sends a deadly freezing beam flying from your fist.

I could have chosen Blinding Sparkle. That's a fantastic bit of wizardry that shoots colorful bedazzling lights into the eyes of monsters. Wicked creatures everywhere pee their pants in fear of the Blinding Sparkle.

Nope. I chose Gas Attack.

SUPERHEROIC ACHIEVEMENT!
Pick a First-Level Spell!
(50 Experience Points Awarded)

Gas Attack allows you to turn anybody, even your-self, into a smelly gas cloud.

The downside with Gas Attack is that you must be touching your victim. This can be slightly tricky when a black dragon is breathing scalding acid all over you and your closest friends. But with that little drawback aside, Gas Attack can occasionally be a fairly handy spell.

But let's be honest. I didn't choose Gas Attack because it's handy.

"Gas Attack?" said Master Elmore. "Hmmm. That's not what I would have suggested. Speak up, boy! Why have you chosen this spell?"

"Well," I said. "You can turn your enemy into a smelly gas cloud."

"That's right," said Elmore the Impressive.

"Basically . . . a fart."

"I . . . suppose," said Elmore the Impressive.

"Come on!" I proclaimed. "That's hilarious!" And I giggled so hard I almost wet myself.

Elmore the Impressive did not find this impressive.

I've been Fart ever since.

CHAPTER TWO

I keep reminding Master Elmore that my name is Bartok. Like right now. We're hiding behind a boulder, peeking out at a yawning cave mouth. We can just see two scruffy goblins guarding the entrance.

"Fart!" Master Elmore hisses. "I said take my spellbook! Quit dillydallying! I have goblins to fight!"

"Sure, Master," I say. "I got your spellbook. Not a problem. And my name is Bartok, remember?"

"What does it matter?" Master Elmore whispers. "You're a useless little assistant!"

I'm not gonna lie, that stings. Right in the feels. "I'm not useless," I mutter.

Master Elmore rolls his eyes. "Oh, my mistake! Perhaps you could flick a booger at the goblins! What a useful contribution that would make to our little group!" Elmore the Impressive can also be Elmore the Super-Sarcastic when he wants to be. "Now SHHH!" he hisses.

"No respect," I grumble.

"It's your own fault," mumbles Pan, polishing her bo staff.

That's Pan Silversnow. An apprentice like me. But an apprentice monk, not an apprentice mage. What's a monk, you ask? Good question. I'm not 100 percent sure. I think it means she fights monsters with only a stick, her fists, and a very serious expression on her face.

Pan looks up from polishing her staff. "How can you expect your master to take you seriously? The first spell you chose was Gas Attack."

I giggle. It's an involuntary reaction. Like breathing. I basically have no choice.

"It's a funny spell!" I say. I poke Moxie in the arm. "Am I right?"

Moxie gives me a playful nudge back. And by "playful

nudge" I mean she sends me flying nostrils-first into the dirt. She turns to Pan. "You gotta admit, it's a funny spell."

Pan shrugs. "Well, now he's a funny boy with a funny spell *and* a funny name."

"I said SHHH!" growls Elmore the Impressive.

I turn my attention back to the business at hand. And by "business" I mean the goblin-slaying, adventure-seeking, treasure-collecting business.

Rumor has it this cave is home to a rampaging pack of about three dozen goblins.

Which is one metric buttload of gob-lins. Obviously.

Master Redmane

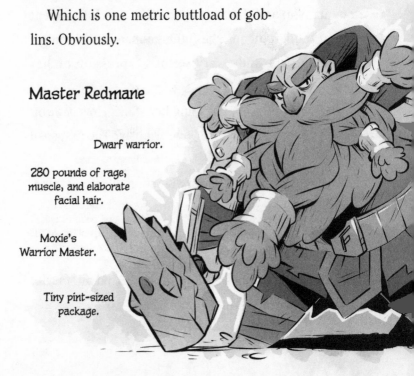

Dwarf warrior.

280 pounds of rage, muscle, and elaborate facial hair.

Moxie's Warrior Master.

Tiny pint-sized package.

That's where me, Pan, Moxie, and our masters—Elmore, Redmane, and Oonah—come in. Our quest? Charge in. Take 'em out. Emerge triumphant.

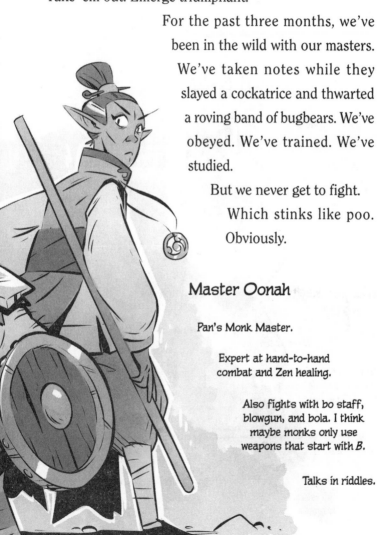

For the past three months, we've been in the wild with our masters. We've taken notes while they slayed a cockatrice and thwarted a roving band of bugbears. We've obeyed. We've trained. We've studied.

But we never get to fight.

Which stinks like poo.

Obviously.

Master Oonah

Pan's Monk Master.

Expert at hand-to-hand combat and Zen healing.

Also fights with bo staff, blowgun, and bola. I think maybe monks only use weapons that start with *B*.

Talks in riddles.

Pan Silversnow

Spiky elf ears.

Spiky elf attitude.

Monk robes and
bo staff.

Never smiles.

Moxie Battleborne

Warrior apprentice.

Can do two hundred push-ups without breaking a sweat.

Walking arsenal of swords and daggers.

Powerhouse of dwarvish brute strength and butt-kicking ability.

Always smiling.

CHAPTER THREE

"You three will hide behind this big boulder," says Master Redmane.

"They're just goblins, Master!" hisses Moxie, yanking a big book from her backpack. *Buzzlock's Big Book of Beasts*. Moxie is never without it. Even back at school, she was the only warrior I ever saw lugging a book around with her everywhere.

"No back talk, ya little guttersnipes!" Master Redmane growls. "A goblin arrow can kill ya just as quick as a dragon!"

Moxie flips to the page on goblins. "*Buzzlock's Big Book of Beasts* says goblins are super easy!"

GOBLIN

Super easy.

"You three aren't ready to battle goblins!" snarls Master Elmore. "You're still inexperienced little nobodies!"

Master Oonah holds up her hand. "Take care from a safe distance and that safe distance will take care of you."

An obedient nod from Pan. Blank stares from me and Moxie. Master Oonah gets a lot of blank stares.

"She means stay here and watch," explains Master Elmore.

"Articulate your observations," says Master Oonah. "Then your observations will be articulate."

"She means we'll quiz you afterward," explains Master Redmane. "If ya answer well, maybe we'll let ya fight in the next battle."

"That's what you said before the *last* battle," Moxie groans. "It's been three months! When are we going to get to fight?"

But the masters are already gone.

There they are, scuttling like sneaky spiders toward the cave. Creeping. Inching. Almost there. And then, Master Redmane's war hammer clanks against the rocks.

SPOTTED!

The first goblin snarls. But it turns into a whimper as he gets a flaming dart to the face, courtesy of Master Elmore.

The second goblin grabs a rusty chain that hangs near the entrance. But Master Redmane's enormous hammer flies through the air.

KLONK!

The goblin hits the ground. Pulling with him . . . the chain.

The three masters spread out as goblins stream from the cave like ants pouring from an anthill. Dozens of them. Maybe hundreds.

"Crud on a cracker," I mutter.

"That's not helpful, Fart," Pan scolds me. "Articulate your observations."

"I observe that there are a ton more goblins than we thought," I say.

"I'm going to help them!" Moxie lunges from our hiding spot.

But Pan places a calming hand on her shoulder. "No," she says. "We were told to wait here."

Moxie grips the handle of her sword anxiously. But she stays put.

The fight is in full swing. Master Elmore and Master Redmane are doing some nice goblin zapping and hammer whacking. But Master Oonah is moving like a mini tornado. Goblins drop right and left before her lightning-fast fists of fury.

And then I spot her.

"Crud on a cracker," I mutter.

"Fart," says Pan sternly. "Articulate your observations."

"Sorry," I say, breathing deeply. "I observe that the goblin in the black robe is a mage."

"*Jiminy-pippity!*" screeches the black-robed goblin. The air around her sparks with red electricity. Her wand starts to glow red. Cracks form along the length of it.

"Stupid goblin," I say. "Something's gone wrong with her spell."

She shakes the wand. Smacks the wand. Whacks the wand against a rock. And that's when–

KA-BLAMMO!

We hit the dirt as an explosion of magical energy fills the air.

Slowly, one by one, Moxie, Pan, and I peek out.

The goblins have been zapped into nothingness! Only their armor and weapons are left.

Yes!

SUPERHEROIC ACHIEVEMENT!
Survive a Goblin Attack!
(100 Experience Points Awarded)

But that's not all. The cave entrance has been blown to bits.

And Master Elmore, Master Redmane, and Master Oonah. They're gone.

Vaporized.

Obliterated.

Disintegrated.

"Cr . . . cr . . . cr . . ." Pan stutters.

"Articulate your observations," I hear myself whisper.

"Crud on a cracker," says Pan.

For once, I agree with the elf.

CHAPTER FOUR

I still remember the first day of school. Headmistress Verbina gathered us all on the Cliffs of Krakentop.

"Welcome to your first day at Krakentop Academy for Heroes," she said. "You are here because you all have the potential to become great heroes."

She said all the usual stuff. Obey your masters. Play

nice with the other kids. Blah-blah-blah. But then she explained wilderness training. "At the end of five years of apprenticeship and study, you and your master will be grouped for Hero Wilderness Training. For one year, your group will journey through the wilds of the Fourteen Realms, righting wrongs, doing daring deeds, and vanquishing evil. Only by completing this year in the wilds . . . and surviving . . . will you graduate from Krakentop and become true heroes."

And so here we are. Three months into our hero wilderness training. We haven't gotten to do much. But it's better than school.

And now . . . our masters are dead. I can't believe it.

We creep out of hiding. There's char and soot everywhere.

"Master Oonah is gone," Pan says, and whispers a chant to the elements.

Moxie mutters a dwarvish prayer of mourning. "Kreorx kaan kladaah." Tears stream from her eyes.

I stare, stunned, at the dark crystal gleaming from the end of Master Elmore's staff. My master is gone. I feel an unexpected tear running down my cheek. All he ever did was call me names, smack me on the ear, and make me trim his toenails. But he was my teacher.

Time passes. Still we stare. Finally, I grit my teeth, bend down, and pick up my master's staff. The crystal pulses purple in response to my touch. Then it fades to darkness.

I clear my throat. "At least the goblins are dead too."

"What are we supposed to do now?" cries Moxie.

Pan lets out a slow breath and shoulders her pack. She grips her bo staff. "If we start now, we can still make some progress before nightfall." She starts walking.

"Where are we going?" asks Moxie.

"Back to Krakentop," says Pan.

"You want to go back to school?" I cry. Yikes. I feel a shiver go down my spine.

I didn't always study magic with Master Elmore. I used to be a farmer's kid. But let's be honest, I wasn't exactly built for farmwork.

My dad's farmworkers used to call me Porkchop instead of Bartok. I was very average at farming. And you know what average gets you in this world? Thrown away. Like garbage.

I think my parents realized that if I were left to take over the farm, we'd probably all starve. So my dad took me to the gates of Krakentop Academy for Heroes. And left me.

Maybe they thought they were doing a good thing.

After all, Krakentop Academy is where nobodies go to become somebodies.

Some students had prepared for entry into Krakentop Academy since birth, like Pan. Most were orphans, like Moxie. Nobody else had been given away by their parents. Just me.

Young Fart

Sort of chubby.

Gets out of breath easily.

Clumsy... Once burned the barn down by accident. Okay, it happened a couple times.

Floppy bird arms are worthless at lifting heavy stuff.

Would-be warriors like Moxie trained at the Kraken-top Battle School, one of the specialized schools within the academy. That wasn't for me.

Apprentice monks like Pan studied meditation and martial arts at the Krakentop Monastery. No good either.

I thought Krakentop was going to throw me out like my parents did. But Master Elmore took a chance on me. "I guess I shall take the round one," he said, pointing at me.

Some of the most famous heroes went here, including Zod the Almighty, Getrick the Grandiose, and Fafner the Highly Flammable.

I couldn't believe it. I was going to become a powerful and mysterious hero! No muscles required!

So I began my studies at the Krakentop High Sanctum of Sorcery.

Guess what I found out—most mages are tall, skinny, and serious. And none of those stick-insect apprentices thought a chubby, short, goofy kid had any business becoming a mage.

The other students were no better. Monks always ate lunch together, looking down their noses at everyone else. Warriors and paladins were even worse. They'd trip you in the hall. Or they sat at the jock table and shot spit wads at the clerics and mages.

Moxie was different . . . She at least nodded when we passed in the halls. Even so, I don't think Pan and Moxie ever said three words to me before we got grouped together for Hero Wilderness Training.

Turns out you can be surrounded by kids your own age and still be totally alone.

For five years, I trained with Master Elmore. I got mostly C-pluses. Guess what a C-plus is?

You got it. Average.

When we left Krakentop Academy for our year of Hero Wilderness Training, I swore to never return. I decided that Bartok the Brilliant would become the most heroic above-average mage who ever lived.

And now Pan wants to go back? Forget it.

CHAPTER FIVE

"Go back to Krakentop?" I exclaim.

Pan sighs deeply. "Isn't it obvious? We need new masters. We need to complete our training."

The thought of stumbling back to Krakentop as a total loser hits me hard. A failure. The thought of those other skinny apprentices laughing at my non-triumphant return.

No way.

A new thought hits me. "What if we didn't go back to Krakentop?" I suggest. "What if we just did this hero thing on our own?"

"That's ridiculous." Pan doesn't even stop walking.

"Okay," I say. I put on my most super-serious voice.

"I just surmised that in your austere wisdom, you would discern the benefits of our current predicament."

This stops her. Big words? Businesslike tone? Calling her "wise" and "austere" and stuff? I'm speaking her language.

"Benefits?" She turns back. "Explain, Fart."

I groan. "Now that Master Elmore is gone, can we please call me Bartok instead of Fart?"

Moxie grimaces. "Gee, Fart. I'm not sure I can get used to that."

Pan raises an eyebrow. "Benefits. Explain."

"Freedom!" I cry, waving my arms in excitement. "We can become the heroes we were always meant to be! No more grades. Nobody holding us back!"

I turn to Moxie. "Do you really want to limp back to school with our tails between our legs? Back to sitting in class? Back to cafeteria food? Everyone will think we couldn't hack it in the wild."

Pan clears her throat. "But the rules . . ."

"Forget the rules for a second!" I cry. "Look. We can always trudge back to school if it doesn't work out. But try and imagine it. Just us! Kicking monster butt and taking monster names! Glory and honor! Real hero stuff!"

"I don't know, Fart," Moxie says, twisting her cloak in her hands. "You heard them. We're still nobodies. Who's going to hire us?"

"We are not nobodies," I say firmly. "We have all the makings of true heroes. What did our masters have that we don't have?"

"Gold?" says Moxie.

"Self-respect?" says Pan.

"Facial hair?" says Moxie.

"Approximately four million experience points?" says Pan.

"No!"

I grab Master Elmore's robes from the ground and pull them on. I strap his spellbook over my shoulder. I lift his staff and strike an impressive wizardly pose.

"Presentation!"

"Cool!" says Moxie. "You look just like Master Elmore!"

"I bet everyone else will think so too," I say.

"What are you suggesting?" asks Pan.

"We dress the part of impressive heroes. If we look impressive, we'll be impressive! I'm not Fart the apprentice," I cry. "I am . . .

Moxie picks up Master Redmane's armor. "You know, I bet this will fit me."

"That's the spirit!" I say and help her with the straps.

"I admit, you look the part," Pan concedes.

"She looks amazing!" I cry. "She is . . .

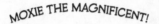

MOXIE THE MAGNIFICENT!

"But let's be honest, Fart," says Pan. "All you know are a few starter spells."

"Experience is the best teacher!" I cry. "I learned the basics at Krakentop. With study and practice, I'll be able to learn all the spells in Master Elmore's spellbook. I swear!"

"Mm-hmm," says Pan. "And what about me?"

"Look at you!" I say. "You're plenty impressive already. It pains me to say it out loud, but I've said it."

Pan smirks. I'm on a roll, so I keep going.

"Add Master Oonah's necklace and fancy ponytail holder and you are . . .

PAN THE PASSIVE-AGGRESSIVE!

"Imagine the challenges we'll face!" I start waving my arms around, painting the picture for her. "You'll become the most skilled monk who ever left Krakentop! And if we do someday return, we'll return as legends."

The hint of a smile shows on Pan's face.

I lower my voice to a whisper. "Not even Master Oonah ever did that."

That's when I know I've got her.

And that's when the rumbling begins.

At the cave entrance, rocks are tumbling. Rubble is raining down. An opening appears.

RAAAAAAAWWWWWWWRRRRRRR!!!

CHAPTER SIX

"GET BEHIND ME!" Moxie roars. She lifts Master Red-mane's war hammer and shield.

Emerging from the cave is the biggest goblin I've ever seen. Then I realize . . . it's not a goblin. This dude is all HOBGOBLIN. He must be the chief of this goblin goon squad. The head honcho. The end boss.

The hobgoblin grips a club the size of a tree trunk. He sends it swinging straight at Moxie and—

BLAMMO!

Her shield goes flying.

But the hobgoblin's not the one making all the rawr-y racket.

He's got an owlbear.

OWLBEAR

Part owl, part
bear (duh).

Ten feet of out-
of-control attitude.

Stinks like decomposing
armpit wrapped
in a rancid tortilla.

Claws that just
won't quit. (Until
you're dead.)

"Do you know any spells?" Pan asks.

"Yes," I say indignantly. "I'm a mage!"

"Besides Fart Attack?"

"Um . . . Feather Friend," I say sheepishly. "I can talk to birds."

"Well, that's going to be perfect if we need to have

a deep, meaningful conversation with a chicken," she says grimly.

I feel about as worthless as a snot sandwich.

"I can also cast Cozy Camp." I hang my head in shame. "It just makes a small campfire."

But Pan's eyes light up. "Do it."

I look at Moxie. She's getting smacked silly by the hobgoblin's monstrous stick-o-doom.

"Do it!" Pan roars.

She startles me back to my senses. I close my eyes and try to remember the words that scuttle from my brain like spiders.

"*Flimmity-flamesh*," I mutter, pointing at a dead branch that lies on the ground.

Instantly, the branch flickers into flame.

Pan yells at Moxie to hit the dirt.

Pan whispers some type of chant, and immediately, my tiny fire roars to life. It multiplies times two . . . times three . . . times ten.

We are suddenly surrounded by a wall of licking flames, an eight-foot-high inferno.

Pan waves her hand and the blaze roars toward the hobgoblin, swallowing him whole.

After a minute, Pan sweeps her hands to snuff out the fire. The ground is covered in wafting smoke. And one crispy-fried hobgoblin.

SUPERHEROIC ACHIEVEMENT!
Defeat a Hobgoblin!
(200 Experience Points Awarded)

Pan and Moxie look at each other and breathe simultaneous sighs of relief.

RAAAAAWWWWWWRRRRRR!

Except we've forgotten a small feathery problem. And when I say "small feathery problem," I mean about a thousand pounds of owlbear.

The owlbear is charging full speed. There's no question ... fancy outfits or not, we're in deep doo-doo.

Then it hits me. Maybe I'm not quite as worthless as a snot sandwich.

"GET BEHIND ME!" I hear myself roar.

Somehow, there's no need to concentrate this time. I find that the words to my Feather Friend spell are instantly on my tongue—

"Pfeatherfax-pfuffernutter!"

I spread my arms and shout "Please! STOP!" Except some kind of hooty, chirpy sound comes out instead.

The owlbear slows down.

"Why should I stop?" roars the owlbear. It's all hoots and tweets to Pan and Moxie, but, magically, I understand every word. Which, let's be honest, feels super cool.

"The bad dude who enslaved you is dead," I say to the owlbear. "You're free."

"Free?" it hoots. "Free as the wind blows?"

"Yeah."

"Free as a summer breeze?"

"Um . . . sure."

"Free as a spring rainfall?"

"I guess."

My first conversation with an owlbear and I get one with the heart of a poet. The piercing owl eyes stare hard at me. "Why not just destroy all of you anyway? I'll still be free."

Gulp. "I guess you could," I hoot. "But let's be honest, that's not gonna end well for any of us."

The owlbear turns to Moxie, who is gripping her hammer ferociously. It sees Pan, poised for action, bo staff at the ready. It turns its jumbo beak back to me and bristles its feathers. "The goblins are all dead?" it asks.

"Yep," I answer.

"Good." It looks at the thicket of trees in the distance and turns back to us. "This is my forest now."

I hold my hands up. "All yours," I say. "Run free. Like the wind and rain and stuff."

The owlbear rears up on its hind legs and lets out a *RAWR!* I brace myself for my imminent gruesome death. But the owlbear turns, shambles into the forest, and disappears.

SUPERHEROIC ACHIEVEMENT!
Sweet-talk an Owlbear!
(100 Experience Points Awarded)

I hear clapping. I turn slowly around. Moxie is applauding me. It's a new sensation. I could get used to this.

Pan relaxes and calmly shoulders her pack. "You know what?"

"What?" I ask.

"I hear experience is the best teacher," she says, almost smiling.

I turn to Moxie. Her goofy smile is even bigger than before.

And so is mine.

Three grinning idiots. That's us.

Because it's official. We are now heroes for hire.

CHAPTER SEVEN

I am so impressed by Pan's magical wall of flame. And I tell her so. Enthusiastically.

But she just stares at me. "I do not use magic." She sits down and pretzel-crosses her legs.

I cannot figure this girl out. "You just made a giant magical fire wall," I point out. "You barbecued a hobgoblin with it."

She looks up. "You misunderstand. A monk draws power from the elements all around us. From the air. Water. Fire. Earth. I cannot *make* fire. I can only manipulate the elements somewhat. The fire must already be there."

"So what you're saying is that my Cozy Camp spell saved your bacon," I say, grinning.

"Your magic spell didn't produce much fire. But I made it work." She starts rummaging through her backpack.

I give her a compliment. She insults my magic. I'd almost think we were starting to figure each other out if my one eye wasn't twitching so bad.

She pulls out a scroll case and unfurls a map.

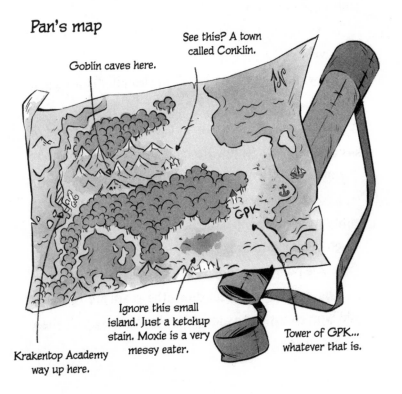

Pan's map

See this? A town called Conklin.

Goblin caves here.

Ignore this small island. Just a ketchup stain. Moxie is a very messy eater.

Krakentop Academy way up here.

Tower of GPK... whatever that is.

"We should head to Conklin," says Pan.

"Good idea," Moxie agrees. "It's the nearest town. A town means food."

"And opportunities for brave heroes like us," I point out. "Towns always have poor dopes that need rescuing."

"Or trolls that need slaying," adds Moxie.

Pan says nothing, but I'm too excited to care. We're heading to Conklin. It's the beginning of our adventure. Nothing can go wrong.

Which is why two days and four hundred foot blisters later, we are completely lost.

"How did you get us lost?" I ask Pan. "You have a map!"

Pan glares at me. "It is not my fault that none of these roads have signs. Perhaps we should have gone the other way back at that fork in the path."

"That was miles ago," I cry in exasperation. Dark, misty woods loom on either side of us. There's nowhere to go but forward or back.

Moxie points ahead of us. "We could ask them."

There, about fifty feet down the road, are two little old women tottering along. I swear they weren't there a second ago.

"If they're out here, they're probably as lost as we are," I tell Pan.

"We are not lost," says Pan. "We simply don't know exactly where we are."

"That's what lost means!"

"Excuse me!" cries Moxie, waving at the old crones. "Hey, ladies?"

"Maybe they're deaf," I say.

Pan reaches out and touches one of their shoulders. "Excuse me, ma'am."

"AAAHHHHH!" the woman screeches at Pan's touch, rounding on us defensively.

"Forgive me, old one," says Pan.

Old is an understatement. She's about four million years old. At least.

"Don't sneak up on an old woman!" she cries.

"What is it, Mathilda?" cries the other, raising her stick. "Spindernots? Grimkins?"

"It's all right, Tabitha," says Mathilda. "It's just these young folk."

"Well, what do they want?" says Tabitha. "Can't they see we're busy?"

"Forgive my sister, young ones. She always gets cranky this time of day," Mathilda says. She pats Tabitha on the arm and motions for her to lower the stick.

"I can hear you, you know," gripes Tabitha.

Mathilda sets her basket on the dusty road. "Now, what can we do for you strangers?" she asks with a snaggletoothed smile.

"We're a bit lost," I say, shooting a look at Pan.

"Lost!" says Mathilda. "Easy place to be in these parts."

"We're trying to get to Conklin," Pan explains.

Mathilda shakes her head. "I'm afraid you missed the road to Conklin many miles ago. You should have turned east a while back."

"Great," I say, plopping down and rubbing my aching

blisters. "Now we have to walk fifteen miles back to that road."

Mathilda picks up her basket. "Well, perhaps we can help you there."

"Wait a minute," says Moxie. "Are you really powerful witches that can teleport us directly to Conklin? That would be so cool!"

Tabitha cackles. "I wish! Do you think I'd be wearing these rags if I were a powerful witch?"

"Shush now, Tabitha," Mathilda says, patting her sister. "There's a small dirt trail through the woods and across the countryside beyond, not far from the clearing where we live. It will save you hours of backtracking."

"It's a shortcut!" squawks Tabitha.

I stand up and smack the dust from my robes. "That sounds perfect," I say. Pan and Moxie nod in agreement.

"This way, then," Mathilda says, hooking her hand into her sister's arm.

She leads us to a break in the trees. Sure enough, a faint dirt trail disappears into the woods beyond.

"We go this way every day to gather roots and herbs," says Mathilda. "It will be nice to have some new company for once."

Soon the forest canopy blocks the sun, leaving us shrouded in dimness.

Pan slows her pace, gesturing for Moxie and me to do the same. Mathilda is gabbing away and seems unaware that we're not listening.

"Are you sure this is a good idea?" asks Pan.

Moxie shrugs, grinning. "They're a couple old ladies," she whispers. "I'm sure we can take them if they try anything."

"Ah, here we are!" says Mathilda.

"I thought you said you lived here," I say. "Don't you have a hut or something?"

Mathilda smiles sweetly. "It's so funny that you thought we were powerful witches, young ones. That just tickles me in my funny bone."

A cold chill comes over me. "You're not, are you?"

"Are you deaf, boy?" squawks Tabitha. "Would I go around wearing these rags if I were a powerful witch?"

Moxie giggles nervously. I look at Pan.

"Now, a powerful harpy," Mathilda says softly. "Well, that's a different thing."

"Oh, if I were a harpy, what else would I wear?" Tabitha croaks. "Especially when these filthy rags make me look so feeble and innocent!"

The old ladies tear the rags from their bodies.

Underneath the robes, they are monstrous.

Claws sprout from their fingertips. Where hoods covered their heads, molting feathers grow instead of hair. Large wings unfold from their backs. But the feet are the worst. Instead of feet, they have oversize bird talons, like gigantic vultures.

CHAPTER EIGHT

Moxie pulls out her hammer as Mathilda and Tabitha soar into the sky. Claws bared, the two harpies attack. Pan and I dive behind the big tree. Moxie slams with her shield and her hammer, but hits nothing except feathers and air.

I turn to Pan. "Cozy Camp?" I ask.

"Why not?" she answers.

It's our new go-to move. It worked great on the hobgoblin—if it ain't broke, don't fix it.

"*Flimmity-flamesh*," I mutter. Some nearby leaves blaze up instantly. Pan manipulates the fire into a small ball of flame and lobs it into the air at Tabitha. The harpy veers to avoid the blaze coming at her. It singes

HARPY

Part lady, part horrifying bird of prey.

Love tricks, riddles, and deception. Their favorite hunting method is to deceive innocent travelers and lead them to their deaths.

Super gross.

At their hearts, they are cowards. They will never fight fair and if they sense they are in real danger, they will always flee.

Often nest in family groups of two or three but there are almost always more close by.

her wing but explodes into a tree, where the wet wood catches fire briefly before sputtering out.

"What are you waiting for?" I pressure Pan. "Light them up!"

"No," Pan answers. "I can't do it without catching the whole forest on fire."

"Good!" I cry. "Burn the creepy place down!"

She snuffs the flame ball out with a flick of her wrist. "I won't do that. These trees have done nothing wrong."

Dang. Foiled by trees.

Moxie gets a good hit with her hammer and Tabitha goes flying across the glade. But the harpy snarls with hate and comes right back for more.

"If you guys have any ideas, now would be a good time," Moxie calls to us.

Pan pulls out her bo staff and prepares to go to Moxie's aid. But then her eye catches something, and she looks down at my waist. "You have a dagger."

I look at my belt. Besides a staff, every mage carries a silver dagger. Mostly for cutting herbs and stuff.

"Yeah?" I say. "So?"

"Throw it," she says, dropping her bo staff.

"Bad idea," I tell her. "Throwing is not my strength. My dad used to refer to my arms as the noodle twins."

Pan takes a deep breath. "We don't have time for this. Do what I said and throw your dagger at the harpies."

"No!" I feel my face flushing. "Think of something else!"

Suddenly talons have Pan by the shoulders.

Mathilda yanks Pan from the ground and soars back into the air, dragging the elf with her like a rag doll.

Ohmygosh. Ohmygosh. Ohmygosh. A paralyzing tightness grips me. This is my fault.

Tabitha cackles with joy and soars toward her sister, claws ready to rip Pan apart.

"Fart, you stubborn human," Pan cries. "Throw. That. Dagger."

I guess looking stupid is better than losing Pan. I pull out my dagger and chuck it at the swooping harpy.

It's a terrible throw, like I knew it would be. But suddenly, an invisible force picks it up and sends my dagger zigzagging through the clearing. I look up and see Pan dangling in midair, making finger gestures like a puppeteer.

The dagger shoots toward Tabitha, who screeches and flaps for cover.

Pan's gestures shift and the wind picks up. The dagger turns sharply and circles Mathilda. She careens through the air, dodging the razor-sharp blade. The dagger stops for a moment, held on the breeze by whatever Pan is doing. Mathilda heads into the forest, leaving us behind and taking Pan with her.

Suddenly, the dagger zips through the air and thunks into Mathilda's back. Screeching, the harpy drops Pan from her grasp and crash-lands on the other side of the clearing.

Tabitha hovers in shock, wings flapping. "MATHILDA!" she cries.

Pan falls, limbs flailing. She nimbly snags a branch and swings herself into a nearby tree.

Tabitha rises into the air. Her face is a grotesque mask of rage. "I'll be back, my little bites!" she screams. "And this time, I'll have all my sisters with me!" She soars through the trees and disappears from sight.

SUPERHEROIC ACHIEVEMENT!
Defeat Some Sneaky Harpies!
(150 Experience Points Awarded)

Pan drops lightly to the forest floor. Moxie lowers her shield and we rush to the wounded elf. Her shoulder bleeds freely from the claws of the harpy. "Pan! Are you okay?" cries Moxie.

Pan pulls wrappings from her backpack and begins bandaging her shoulder. "Yes. I'm all right."

"What did you do?" I ask. "How did my dagger zig around like that?"

Pan knots her bandage tightly. "Fire isn't the only thing I can manipulate," she says with a smirk. "Wind is an element too, you know."

Moxie blows out a breath of relief and starts laughing. "I don't know what you did, but you got Mathilda good!" She stomps through the brush to where the harpy fell.

"I can't believe that," I say, still a little stunned. "They almost got you."

"Yes, they almost did," she says, her pointed eyebrows raised at me. "So the next time I tell you to throw your dagger, throw it."

That's elvish sass right there. I nod but remain silent.

Moxie clomps back with my dagger in her hand. "Good shot," she tells Moxie. "It's too bad Fart didn't have two daggers. You could have taken out Tabitha too."

"Tabitha!" I cry. "She's coming back with more of those things! We should get out of here!"

"Not before I check this tree for treasure," says Moxie. She's already climbing toward the big nest. "Hey, you guys! There's a small chest up here. Let's open it!"

"No!" I cry. "We've got to get out of here!"

"Okay," says Moxie. "It's little. We can bring it with us." She jumps down with a box in her hands.

Pan picks up her bo staff. "Tabitha knows we're heading to Conklin. They'll be waiting for us back on the road. We should cut across the countryside. And we should move quickly." She darts through the trees, leaping nimbly over a fallen log.

I shrug at Moxie. We lumber after her, putting as much distance as we can between us and the harpy lair.

CHAPTER NINE

We emerge from the misty forest. A small cluster of trees looms in the distance, but other than that, it's all prairie and high grass. I keep looking nervously behind me, but there's no sign of the harpies.

I brush off Moxie's cloak. "Ick. You're covered in feathers and harpy schmutz," I tell her.

"Speaking of feathers, let me see your spellbook," she says. "I want to try casting that Feather Friend spell."

I laugh. "Magic doesn't work like that," I tell her. "You don't just read the spells out of the book. You couldn't even read the words. See?"

"Whoa," she says. "You can read that?"

I nod. "But it's very complicated and easy to mess up. I have to study it until I have the words just right. And sometimes there are complicated gestures."

"Less talking, more walking, if you please," Pan calls back to us.

"Can we slow down?" I ask.

"We need cover," says Pan, nodding ahead of us. "I would like us to reach that grove of trees before dark."

"How about a short rest then?" says Moxie, huffing

and puffing. "These little legs of mine were not meant for this kind of hustle."

Pan stops. "Yes, five or ten minutes would be fine." She pulls out her map and looks across the countryside.

Moxie plops the little chest to the ground. "And," she says with a grin, "as long as we're stopped, we can open up this baby." She tugs at the lid, but it won't budge.

"You'll need a key to open that," says Pan, looking up from her map. She points to the front of the box.

"I've got the key," Moxie says, holding up her hammer.

"No! Don't . . ." Pan begins.

THE HARPY BOX

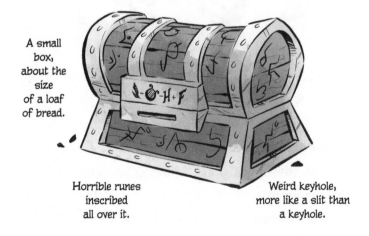

A small box, about the size of a loaf of bread.

Horrible runes inscribed all over it.

Weird keyhole, more like a slit than a keyhole.

But Moxie's already swinging with all her might.

BAM!

I look down, ready to see the chest smashed to bits. But it's still in one piece. And still locked.

"Weird," Moxie says. "That usually works."

"It's probably magically protected," says Pan. "Like I said, you'll need a key."

"Did you see a key on Mathilda?" I ask Moxie.

"Nope," she says. "Just your dagger."

And then I notice that written above the keyhole are little symbols:

"There are little pictures on here," I point out. "What the heck is that first one?"

"Let me see," says Pan. She inspects the engraving closely. "That is heatherharp."

"Heatherharp?" I ask, shaking my head. "What's heatherharp?"

"Heatherharp is a plant. Obviously."

I squint at the little symbol. "How do you know it's heatherharp?"

Moxie laughs. "Elves practically worship nature. If Pan says that's heatherharp, it is."

"Thank you," says Pan, turning back to her map.

Moxie, scratches her head. "But what does heatherharp have to do with this cute little guitar?"

"I don't think that's a guitar," I point out. "I've seen those before. It's like a xylophone. No, a harp! It's a harp!"

"Hey, just like in heatherharp!" says Moxie. So, heatherharp-dash-harp-dash-*H*-plus-*F*."

It hits me like a flash. "Not dash. Minus! Heatherharp minus harp!" I cry.

"That leaves just plain old heather," says Moxie.

"Right!" I'm getting excited now. "And plain old heather minus *H*?"

"Um . . . 'eather'?" Moxie asks.

"Exactly!" I jump up and down. Pan has looked up from the map with interest. "Plus *F*! What does 'eather' plus *F* equal?"

Moxie shakes her head. "A headache?"

I smile. "'Eather' plus *F* is . . ." I reach out and pluck a long harpy feather from Moxie's cloak. "Feather!"

I insert the feather into the slot. There's a click. And the lid slowly opens.

SUPERHEROIC ACHIEVEMENT!
Open a Tricky Chest!
(50 Experience Points Awarded)

"Of course," says Pan, looking impressed. "A harpy's magic chest, designed so only a harpy can open it. It's really rather brilliant."

"Nice one, Fart!" grins Moxie.

The chest holds a small pouch, a sparkly bracelet, and a ring.

Moxie grabs the pouch, yanks the drawstrings, and dumps it out into her hand. Gold coins gleam from her palm.

"Now, THAT's what I'm talking about!" she cries. "There's gotta be fifty or sixty gold pieces in here!"

Pan reaches for the bracelet. The diamonds sparkle merrily in the sunlight. "While elves do not share the love of gold that dwarves have, we do love diamonds." She gazes into the gems. I've never seen her like this. "They reflect the light of the stars and the spirit of the earth all in one."

I snort. "Yeah. That's why you like diamonds. For spiritual reasons." I reach into the box and pull out the ring. It is an intertwined band of silver metal. A blue stone, like an eye, shines from the top.

I slide it onto my finger.

Immediately, I notice a change. A blue glow starts to shine from my staff! I drop it to the ground and step back.

"What's wrong?" Moxie asks.

"My staff started glowing. The chest is glowing too!" I cry. "And this ring!"

"Interesting," says Pan thoughtfully. "We know this chest is enchanted, because Moxie could not smash it open. And your staff is obviously a magical creation . . . We have seen Master Elmore do many magical feats with it."

"Your hammer is glowing blue too," I tell Moxie.

"Master Redmane always said that his hammer was enchanted with the power to hit twice as hard as he alone could," says Moxie.

"That confirms it, then," says Pan. "You have found a ring of magic detection."

Moxie holds her hand out. "Let me try!" she says. "I want to see the glow."

I pull the ring off and the blue auras disappear. Moxie squeezes the ring onto her stubby finger. "I don't see any glow," she says, disappointed.

"Let me try," says Pan, reaching for the ring. She puts it on. "Nothing. Perhaps this ring only works on the hand of a mage."

"Cool," I say, sliding the ring back onto my finger. The blue glows return, twinkling brightly.

"That's one very nice bit of treasure for each of us," says Pan, hooking the bracelet onto her wrist.

"And don't forget this awesome chest," says Moxie, stuffing the box and the feather into her backpack.

SUPERHEROIC ACHIEVEMENT!
Get Some Sweet Treasure!
(50 Experience Points Awarded)

A noise carries on the wind behind us. The cry of a bird. Or a bird-lady.

"We need to get going," says Pan.

"Yes, please," I say, scanning the horizon nervously.

"There's a problem, however," she says, holding up her map. "I can't find the road."

"What?" I cry. "But Mathilda said that if we cut across the countryside, it would lead us to the road to Conklin."

"Yes, Fart," says Pan. "Mathilda also tried to eat us."

"So . . . we're lost?" I ask. "Again?"

I stand and stumble on the bottom of my robes. Dumb old robes. Dumb old Pan.

"How are we lost?" Moxie asks. "You have a map."

Dumb old map.

"I need a point of reference," Pan says. "Something to show me exactly where we are on the map. A mountain. An odd tree."

"You're an odd tree," I mutter.

Pan scans the horizon, fidgeting absently with her necklace. Finally, she points. "We should head that way. Toward that tower."

I hadn't noticed it before, but she's right. Sticking above a nearby grove of trees. The pointy top of a tower.

"How do you know we should go that way?" I ask.

She tucks her necklace into her tunic. "I just do."

Moxie peers at Pan's super-unhelpful map. "That must be the Tower of GPK."

"Okay, what's a GPK?" I ask. "And do they eat mages? Because I'm tired of running for my life."

"Why don't we ask them?" suggests Moxie. Four large people burst from the trees. And they're being followed . . . or chased . . . by a smaller figure. Something not human.

"Do not go!" cries the tiny figure. "Think about all them riches! Think about what this quest gonna do for your reputation!"

Reputation? Riches? Quest? I look sharply at Moxie and Pan. We're in the market for all three of those things.

As the four figures approach, there's no doubt: These are mighty heroes! It's easy to see. Their armor gleams! Their weapons shine! Their chins are sharp and strong!

Also, they are yelling, "WE ARE MIGHTY HEROES!"

The small creature chasing after them looks like a frog man. Or a gecko guy. Blue skin with black spots. Slimy. Wearing a tool belt full of jangling metal gizmos. You know the type.

"Our reputation is what we're worried about!" says the first burly hero.

"Aye, tiny amphibian creature!" says the second. "Tell your master we are not the heroes he seeks!"

"Don't you know who we are?" says the third. "We are the elite!"

"We are the mighty!" chimes in the fourth.

"Yes, yes," says the frog man wearily. "You already spoke this to TickTock . . ."

But they raise their voices in unison anyway.

"Hey, guys!" I interrupt. "Could you tell us how to get to Conklin—"

And that's when Chico's chest slams smack into my highly breakable face. It's like getting run over by a six-foot bucket of boulders.

"Move aside, feeble runts," says Chico. He wads up a piece of parchment, throws it at my head, and steps over me like I'm a sack of rotten cabbages.

"Hey!" yells Moxie. She helps me to my feet. "Don't you know who this is? This is . . . BARTOK THE BRILLIANT!"

I remember to strike a majestic pose just in time.

This gets their attention.

All four pause. All four look. All four yawn.

"Never heard of him," says Chico. "But that's a splendid battle hammer! From whence did you acquire it, short girl-child?"

Moxie stutters for an answer. "From . . . my . . ."

"Yes?" says Chico.

I jump in. "From the treasure trove of . . . a dragon!"

Chico lets out a belly laugh. "I doubt that!" he chortles. "Your garb is choice, your weapons impressive, but no seasoned heroes are ye, wee children!" He turns and walks away.

"Stand aside, ye diapered infants!" says Gorgothar, pushing past.

They push past us and amble into the distance, lifting their voices in song about the glories of the magnificent Man-Bun Brotherhood.

I can't deny it. It's impressive. Four-part harmony like that is no joke.

The frog man wrings his slender hands. "Now what TickTock gonna do?" he cries. "Master is gonna be so mad!" He turns and trudges back toward the tower.

I pick up the wad of parchment and unwad it. I read. And I grin.

"TickTock," I call after the frog man. "Let your master know that his heroes have arrived."

"What are you talking about?" Moxie asks. She grabs the parchment and gives it a once-over.

Pan takes a peek. "Am I the only one who sees the little skulls on that paper?"

"Maybe this is our ticket to glory and honor," I say. I step boldly forward . . . and trip on my robes.

Pan slowly massages her temples. "This is not going to end well."

CHAPTER TEN

The frog man leads us into the tower. Weird mechanical gadgets whir and buzz from every surface. My heart pounds with excitement.

"Hey, little frog man," says Moxie, reaching out to touch a spinning gizmo. "Whose tower is th . . . OW!"

He smacks her hand. "No touch!" he shouts. "Tick-Tock not a frog. And definitely not a man."

"Sorry," says Moxie sheepishly. "You probably hate when people make that mistake. You're obviously a gecko."

"Not a gecko," he says.

"Toad thingy?"

"Not a toad, not a salamander, not a fish," he says.

"TickTock is a phibling. And TickTock's name is TickTock."

TICKTOCK

About two feet tall.

Tool belt full of shiny metal contraptions.

Hates being called a frog. Really hates being called a man.

Pan steps in. "TickTock, whose tower is this?"

"Will see very soon," says TickTock. "Stay here." He flaps up the stairs and disappears from sight.

"Fart..." Pan begins.

"You mean Bartok?" I correct her.

"Whatever," she sighs. "Did it ever occur to you that those Man-Bun guys probably turned down this job for a reason?"

"Those four goobers?" says Moxie. "They're probably just chicken."

Pan twirls her hair-wispies nervously. "Chico and company looked like a lot of things. But chicken wasn't one of them."

Moxie deflates a bit. "We also didn't fool them with our brave hero act."

"We just need to sell it better," I cry. "It's all about presentation!"

"Maybe we're in over our heads," says Pan. "Maybe we should head back to Krakentop."

"Just be cool!" I say. "I'm sure it'll be fine!"

"Famous last words," mutters Pan.

TickTock comes padding down the stairs. "Brave heroes!" says the phibling.

It takes me a second to realize that he's talking to us. "Oh! Yep! Right here!"

TickTock bows formally. "TickTock presents his master to you."

A staff thumps on the stairs.

"The Mystical!" says TickTock. "The Perplexing!"

Pan turns to Moxie. "Did he just say *Kevin*?"

"WHO BEGS AN AUDIENCE WITH THE GREAT AND POWERFUL KEVIN?" he booms.

I hold up the parchment. "We're here about your help-wanted ad," I squeak.

The wizard throws his hood back and looks at us like something gross he just stepped in. "Oh, come *on!*" he bellows. "TickTock, you doofus! Them?"

I can see now that he's more tubby than towering. His hair sticks out in all directions like he just woke up from a nap.

"KEVIN!!!" A voice screeches from one of the upper chambers. "WHO'S AT THE DOOR?"

Kevin hangs his head. "Nobody! Just my friends! Okay?"

He turns to us. "Don't be alarmed. It's just my pet imp."

"I HEARD THAT, YOUNG MAN!!!"

"Quit listening to my private conversations!" he screams up the stairs. "Gosh!"

TickTock tugs on his robes. "But Master, the Man-Bun Brotherhood says no! TickTock is getting these heroes instead!"

Kevin snatches the parchment and holds it out to the

tiny phibling. "TickTock. Buddy. Pal. There's a reason I used the word 'mighty' twice! I'm looking for heroes, not preschool knuckleheads."

"Hey!" says Moxie, standing up tall and flexing her forearms. "We're mighty!"

"Yeah!" I say, a little less squeaky than before. "And we're heroes!"

"And only one of us is a knucklehead," says Pan softly, her eyes darting at me.

"That's nice, kiddies," says Kevin. "The answer is no." He grabs me by the shoulder and ushers me toward the door.

But Moxie grabs his wrist and raises her hammer defensively. "There's no need to push my friends," she says coldly. "We're going."

Kevin stares at her. At us. He seems to be deciding something. I hope it's not whether or not to melt our faces with a fireball. He steps back, an amused look plastered across his face.

"Hmm. Maybe you three are just what I'm looking for," Kevin says thoughtfully.

"See?" I whisper to Pan. "It's all about selling it!"

The Great and Powerful Kevin paces in front of us,

his staff thumping loudly on the wooden floor with each step.

"So, tell me, heroes. Are you brave?"

Moxie clangs her hammer against her shield. "The bravest."

"I hope so," he says. "'Cuz you're hired. Follow me."

SUPERHEROIC ACHIEVEMENT!
Get a Job!
(150 Experience Points Awarded)

CHAPTER ELEVEN

Kevin the Great and Powerful leads us behind a curtain. I try hard not to trip on my robes. Everything seems really breakable.

"Gather around," he whispers.

Kevin looks all super mysterious in the candlelight. The guy clearly knows the power of presentation. I mentally take notes on his wizardly stage presence. This stuff is gold.

He whips a cloth from a long table to reveal an open book and a map. His voice is barely a whisper. "About twelve leagues due south from here is a village called . . . uh . . . yes?"

I've raised my hand. I have an important question.

"How far is a league?"

Kevin sighs. "I dunno. A good ways."

"Is it like a mile?" I ask. "More? Less?"

"Does it really matter right now?"

"We get lost a lot. These details could be important."

"Sheesh." He turns to the phibling. "TickTock?"

"Twelve leagues is being like two and a half days of walking," says TickTock.

"There," says Kevin, turning back to me. "Okay? Would it be better if I just said 'a two-and-a-half-day walk'?"

"Yep." I smile. "Super helpful."

Kevin glares at me with his Great and Powerful eyes. "Can I get back to my story now?"

"You betcha," I say. "It's really great so far. Keep going."

Kevin the Annoyed and Flustered takes a breath and starts over. "About a two-and-a-half-day walk south of here is a village called Taterhaven. Past the village are the Foothills of Bumble and in these hills are the Caves of Catastrophe. Don't even get me started on all the horrible beasts that live in these caves."

Kevin turns the page in his book. "But chief among them is a tribe of really savage ogres.

"These ogres," Kevin continues, "guard a rare creature."

He points to his book. It says *the golden* . . . something. It's kinda smudgy.

"What's that say?" asks Moxie. "I can't read your handwriting."

OGRE

Not green or friendly, despite stories you may have heard.

Will eat humans or vegetables, but their favorite meal is donkey. Who knew?

About nine feet tall.

Says "duh" a lot. Like, a whole lot.

"I'll tell you what it says," Kevin whispers. "It says . . . 'the golden llama.'"

Pan tilts her head at Kevin. "The rare creature is a golden *llama*?"

Kevin nods. "Yep. I'm guessing it has solid-gold hair or something."

"Solid-gold hair!" I rub my hands together. "I like the sound of that."

"So," says Moxie, "you want us to barge in there, slay this golden llama, and bring its gold fur back to you."

"No slaying the llama!" he says. "Not unless you wanna fight a bunch of seriously cheesed-off ogres."

I shake my head at Kevin. "I don't get it. You don't want us to slay the llama. You don't want us to slay the ogres. What is this quest?"

Kevin looks sharply into my eyes. "Sneak in, get what I need, and bring it back to me."

Pan raises an eyebrow. "And what is this thing we're supposed to acquire?"

"I know!" says Moxie. "You want us to bring you the llama hair!"

"No," says Kevin.

"The wool."

"No."

"The fleece."

"No."

"The fur."

"Quit saying different words for hair!" cries Kevin. "I do not want you to bring me the golden llama's hair!"

I look at Moxie and Pan. They seem just as confused as I am. "Then what?" I ask.

Kevin looks at us each in turn. "I want you to bring me . . ."

"Yes?" says Pan.

". . . the llama's . . ."

"Yes?" says Moxie.

". . . golden . . ."

"Yes?" I say.

". . . gas."

There's silence. For, like, a full minute. I try hard to understand. "The llama's golden . . . gas?"

I want to giggle. I really do. But I am stunned into silence.

But Pan is unfazed. "You need us to bring you a golden llama's fart?"

"Yes!" says Kevin. "Like, a really loud, juicy one. A seriously explosive llama fart."

"Uh-huh," says Pan.

"Uh-huh," says Moxie.

"Uh-huh," says me. We're all thinking it. Kevin the Great and Powerful is actually Kevin the Cuckoo for Cocoa-Puffs.

"What do you need llama gas for?" asks Pan.

Kevin doesn't answer. He walks over to one of the nearby bubbling flasks. Smells it. Removes the flame from underneath it. "It's . . . an ingredient."

"For what?" asks Pan.

"None of your beeswax!" says Kevin. "I just need it! Okay?"

"Well, cut the cheese and put it on a cracker!" says Moxie. "Fart! This quest has your name written all over it!"

"You're right," says Pan solemnly. "It's as if the winds of fate are moving before us."

But I spot a serious problem. "Are we just supposed to sit around and wait for it to rip one? That could take forever."

Kevin brings over a small chest and sets it before us. "Already solved that problem," he says, grinning. Slowly, ceremoniously, he opens the lid and lifts out a small silk-wrapped bundle.

"What's that?" I ask.

"A one-of-a-kind artifact," he says. "My own concoction."

We lean in eagerly. "Is it an amulet?" asks Pan. "Some sort of diamond?"

"A golden axe?" Moxie asks hopefully.

"Better." Kevin unwraps the silk cloth. "I call it . . . the Bean Burrito of Destiny."

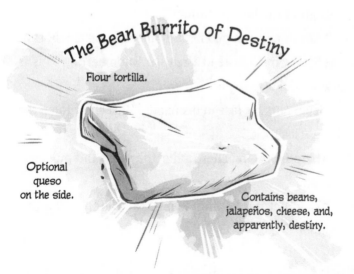

The Bean Burrito of Destiny

Flour tortilla.

Optional queso on the side.

Contains beans, jalapeños, cheese, and, apparently, destiny.

I get chills. Literal goose bumps up and down my arm.

"Just feed this to the creature," says Kevin. "In ten minutes, that llama will be squeezing cheese like there's no tomorrow."

Moxie steps in for a closer look at the mighty magical burrito. "How are we supposed to transport a llama fart to you?"

The mage turns to the phibling. "My lackey will explain."

TickTock bristles. "Not lackey. We spoked about this."

"Servant, then," says Kevin.

"Not servant."

Kevin grins sheepishly. "You're making me look bad in front of the heroes, flunky."

"Not flunky, not peon," says the phibling stubbornly. "Assistant in Charge of Creative Engineering. This is title we did discussing."

Kevin puts his face in his hands. "Just show them the thing, TickTock."

The phibling reaches under the table and pulls out a bottle.

"TickTock's invention," he says proudly. "The Gas Trapper™!"

"Wait a second," says Moxie, gagging a little. "We have to stick that bottle in the llama's . . . y'know . . . golden gas place?"

TickTock sighs with exasperation. "Not sticking it in!" he says. "Sticking it *near*!" He turns the bottle over. There's some kind of gizmo built into the bottom.

"A fan," says TickTock. "Wait for llama to . . . you know . . ."

"Squeak one out?" Moxie says.

"Play the butt trumpet?" I say.

"Toot?" Pan says.

"YES!" says TickTock. "Wait for the llama to do the toot. Put the end of the bottle near the toot place and then you are pressing the button. The toot is being sucked into the bottle by this fan, and presto!"

"Fart in a bottle," I say, wonderstruck. "It's pure genius."

Kevin slides the Bean Burrito of Destiny across the table. TickTock hands the Gas Trapper™ to Moxie. I pull out the harpy box and place them gingerly inside.

SUPERHEROIC ACHIEVEMENT!

Acquire a Super-Powerful
Artifact!

(100 Experience Points Awarded)

Kevin stands up to his full height. "Bring me that which I seek and I'll reward you nicely."

There's no question. My whole life has been leading up to this moment. So I say the only five words you can say at a time like this:

CHAPTER TWELVE

It's the second night of our two-and-a-half-day walk, and we are gathered around one of my Cozy Campfires. Beyond the glow of the fire, wolves howl.

Pan is off to the side, legs crossed, eyes closed. Communing with the elements. But Moxie and I have been having the mother of all burping contests.

Poof! I disappear into a cloud of gas.

Gas Attack. It's a beautiful spell.

Moxie's rolling in the dirt, howling with laughter. I let her enjoy herself for a few moments, and then I release the spell and flump back into my natural form.

"You . . . you . . ." Moxie is gasping for breath through her laughter. Tears stream down her face. "You turned yourself into a fart!"

"Beat that," I say.

Moxie applauds. "I yield to the master!"

I'm soaking in my not-so-sweet-smelling victory when a shadow falls over us.

It's Pan. I didn't see her get up. "What is wrong with you?" she snaps, her eyes piercing the darkness.

Moxie holds up her hands in apology, her face still red from laughing. "I'm sorry, Pan. You're trying to meditate, and we're making all this racket."

"It's not the noises," she says, gathering her robes around her indignantly. "It's not even the smells." She points to me. "It's you."

"Me?" I'm the picture of innocence.

"You do not take your magic seriously," she says coldly.

"Sheesh, Pan," I say. "Lighten up. Besides, what do you know about it?"

"Plenty," she says softly. "My mother was a mage. A great one. She died because a lesser mage in her party wasn't paying attention. Wasn't taking things seriously."

Moxie stops giggling. The mood around the campfire has definitely shifted. I stare at the ground.

"You have limitless possibilities at your fingertips," says Pan. "Yet you treat your gift like a joke."

"What are you even talking about?" I ask, shooting her a look. She turns to me, glaring.

"You could have picked any early spells you wanted! You could shoot flaming darts from your fingertips! You could make your enemies fall asleep with a snap! But no. You pick Butt Bubble."

"It's called Gas Attack!" I say.

"And Feather Friend!" she says with dripping sarcasm.

"That actually came in pretty handy," Moxie mutters.

"He got lucky," says Pan.

"Lucky?" I ask indignantly. My face starts to get hot.

"If that had been just a bear instead of an owlbear, you would have been helpless," she says. "When it comes time to fight, Moxie swings her hammer with skill and I bring enemies down with fire, air, and fist. And you watch. Helpless."

I stutter to defend myself. "I . . . I . . . I'll have you know that I've been studying Master Elmore's spellbook every night."

"Yeah," says Moxie, rushing to my defense. "You've probably learned several new spells already, right?"

"Um, no," I say sheepishly. "But I'm making progress on a new spell. A good one!"

Pan's face is made of stone. "What's the spell called?" she asks.

I wad my robes in my fists. "It doesn't matter what it's called!"

"What's it called?" she asks again. "Something funny. Right?"

I grit my teeth. "It's called Puppy Power. Okay? It turns whoever I cast it on into a cute little puppy!"

"Of course it does," says Pan.

"Something can be useful and hilarious at the same time, you know!" I yell.

A noise comes from the edge of the firelight. We all turn.

"Nice job, loudmouth," says Pan. "You've attracted a wolf."

But this sound is no wolf. It's a squishy burrowing sound, like the noise of the world's biggest gopher. A few feet away, a mound of dirt rises from the ground. We back away nervously. A hole appears. And then we see it, emerging from the hole.

A huge slithering body. And a mouth. No, two mouths.

Crud on a cracker . . . Three mouths.

Moxie grabs her hammer. "Oh, yuck," she says grimly. "That's a slithering wormer."

It glides toward us on a trail of slime, mouths snapping ferociously in our direction.

Moxie rushes in, clobbering the creature in its worm face and leading it away from the rest of us. The wormer chomps at her, but she manages to duck the beaklike jaws.

Pan leaps over the fire and swings her bo staff hard at the tail. Her staff just bounces off the blubbery body. The tail lashes out, knocking Pan back toward the fire.

SLITHERING WORMER

Giant 15-foot worm.

Three mouths. One inside the other... inside the other. Disgusting.

Great bait for fishing, but you need a really big hook.

Moxie manages to get two or three really good poundings in with her hammer, slowing down the enormous slithering beast.

Pan reaches out toward the campfire. Tongues of flame leap up from the fire and strike out at the tail of the beast. The slimy mucus on its skin sizzles, and the wormer lets out a monstrous howl. It turns to snap at Pan with its mouths, but she flips backward out of the way.

My chest tightens with fear. I grab my staff and crawl away from the creature, putting the campfire between myself and the wormer.

The slithering wormer suddenly decides this meal is too much trouble. It screeches toward the heavens and slithers quickly back down its hole, leaving a puddle of flaming goo behind.

SUPERHEROIC ACHIEVEMENT!
Scare Off a Slithering Wormer!
(150 Experience Points Awarded)

I'm still kneeling by the fire, gripping my staff defensively. "Good job, you guys," I say.

Pan turns to me. "Don't bother getting up, Fart," she says coldly. "We'll handle everything."

I feel all my anger surging back to the surface. "I'm a mage!" I cry. "I'm supposed to hang back behind the fighters. That's how it works!"

Pan just shakes her head. "Master Elmore was a mage. You are no mage, Fart." She turns away in a swirl of robes.

"My name is BARTOK!" I shout at her back.

I pick up a stick and stab ferociously at the fire.

"She doesn't mean it," Moxie whispers, sitting back down. "She's just tired. We all are. We lost our masters just a few days ago. We've walked more miles than I can count. We're getting attacked by giant worms." She bites her bottom lip and stares into the fire. "She's just tired."

I'm so furious, I could spit. Pan is so stuck up! But it's more than that.

Because deep down, I'm nervous. Nervous that maybe she's right.

CHAPTER THIRTEEN

The next day, we mostly walk in silence. Moxie tries to smooth out the tension, but her good-natured jokes fall flat and she finally gives up.

It's late afternoon. It's already turning dark, and a storm is blowing in when we find ourselves standing on the edge of a valley, looking down upon a village. Taterhaven.

"Well, we're not here to sightsee," says Pan. "Let's find an inn and get out of the rain. We'll head to the Caves of Catastrophe first thing in the morning. We have intestinal gas to collect."

I grip the staff in my hand. Master Elmore's staff.

I have seen him do amazing magic with this staff, its purple crystal glowing with power. But the crystal isn't glowing anymore. Maybe it only glows at the touch of a real mage. Maybe the staff knows that Pan is right.

By the time we get into town, the rain shower has turned

into a full-blown storm. The wind whips my robes, and the street has turned to mud.

"Look!" Moxie points. "There's the inn."

The Yam's Pajamas. There's a picture on the sign of a giant orange potato wearing a bathrobe. It's super weird. But it's not the weirdest sign we see.

Nailed to the door is a wanted poster.

We are greeted by a cozy fire inside. Lots of the tables are already filled with rugged burly strangers. They give us nervous glances, then turn back to their mugs.

We grab an empty table in the corner and sit down.

A lady comes over to us. She wears a wide smile and a grimy apron. "Hey, there, strangers! Welcome to the Yam's Pajamas. My name's Taro. What'll you have?"

"What do you have?" asks Moxie.

"What do we have?!" Taro cries in alarm.

The room goes silent.

"Where do you people think you are?" asks Taro.

"Um . . . Taterhaven," says Moxie.

"Exactly! So what do you think we serve?"

"Um . . ." Moxie thinks for a second. "Taters?"

"Now you're catching on!" says Taro with a big grin.

Everybody laughs.

"Be sure to try the mashed taters!" says a guy at the next table.

"No, no, no, Russet," pipes in a lady. "They should get the boiled taters."

"You're crazy, Fennel," says a tall guy. "The baked tater is king at the Yam's Pajamas!"

We look at Taro. "I guess we're having taters," I say. "Spiced for me."

"Baked," says Moxie.

"Boiled," says Pan.

She starts to leave. "Oh, yeah," Moxie says. "We'll also need some food for the road."

"Not a problem, strangers. I've got some fried tater chips that stay good for weeks. Perfect for adventurer types!"

We sit quietly for a minute, soaking in the warmth from the fire.

Pan tugs at her hair-wispies and turns to me. "I want to apologize for my words last night."

Moxie slaps me on the back. "See? I told you she didn't mean it!"

"Oh, no. I meant what I said."

"Oh, that's just great," I mumble. "Apology not accepted." I turn away with a huff. "Why do you have to be so snobby?"

"I am not snobby," she says.

"Yes, you are. Back at school, you wouldn't even talk to me. Always so above it all!"

"It's not because I'm snobby," she says.

"Oh, then it's just me personally who's inferior to you?" I say. "Much better."

"No! It's just . . ."

"What?"

"I'm an elf!" she cries. "Elves live for thousands

of years. It's not easy to make friends with non-elves, because . . ."

"Because why?" I exclaim, bristling with frustration. "Because everyone else is beneath you?"

"Because they're going to die someday!" she cries. "Why get to know someone when you're just going to lose them?"

I let this sink in. I have to admit, I never thought of it like that.

Pan takes a deep breath. "Look, I meant the things I said. But I said them in a really mean way," she says. "I'm sorry for that."

Moxie nudges me. "See? She's sorry, man."

Pan releases her hair and folds her hands on the table. "Our lives are in each other's hands, at least for this quest. That means we're going to have to trust each other. You can't trust me if you are mad at me."

I wait for more. "And?"

Pan's eyes dart up to mine. "And I can't trust you if I continue to doubt you. Yes, you picked some dumb spells on your spell-picking day."

"Hey!" I cry. Maybe it's true. But still. Hey.

She cuts me off. "But you have used what little you have for the good of the group. I should not doubt your commitment to your magic or our group just because you are very different than me."

I eyeball her, looking for some sign that she's messing with me. But she seems to mean it. "You trust me?"

She nods. "I shall try to."

I bite my bottom lip. I can tell Moxie's holding her breath, eager to put this behind us. I look at Pan. Her pointy ears. Her pointy nose. Her pointy eyebrows. Even her topknot somehow manages to be pointy. I realize that it must be hard for someone this pointy to even try to trust somebody as soft and squishy as me.

I slowly reach my hand across the table. "Okay," I say.

Pan shakes my hand. "Okay."

Moxie releases a huge sigh of relief. "OKAY!" She grins broadly. "Taro! Give us three big glasses of chocolate milk over here! We're celebrating!"

"Hooray!" cry all the farmers, raising their mugs to toast us.

I turn to a nearby table. "So," I say. "What's the deal with that wanted poster on the door?"

Room silent. Warmth gone. Laughter evaporated. It only took me about two and a half seconds to kill the celebration.

Oh well. At least there's chocolate milk.

CHAPTER FOURTEEN

Russet marches to the door and rips off the wanted poster. "That there is Tim and Steve," he says. "A two-headed terror that plagues our peaceful village."

"He's a beast!" says Fennel. "He leads a whole band of boogers up in them caves!"

"Boogers?" Moxie snickers. "I think you mean ogres."

"What have they done?" asks Pan.

"Raided us peaceful folk to satisfy their fiendish appetites," cries Russet.

"Whoa! They ate . . . some people?" whispers Moxie.

"Worse!" cries Taro. "They took our taters!"

"Did you see the storehouse when you came up?" asks Russet.

"Them boogers broke in," says Fennel. "They busted it all up and made off with loads of our precious taters!"

"Gosh," says Moxie. "That's terrible."

"That Tim and Steve carries a huge mace. He puts a fresh notch in the handle for every sack of taters he steals," says Russet. "It's a crime, I tell you!"

"We need that Tim and Steve gone," says Fennel. "That'll send the rest of them boogers running for the hills."

"Fat chance," says Russet. "Remember that group that went to the caves last year? Disappeared forever!"

"And those barbarians who went this past spring?" says Fennel. "Never heard from them again."

"We had a group of heroes leave for them caves just a few days ago," says Russet. "We'll probably never see them again either."

Taro shows up with our dinner. "Darker tales for other nights!"

she says. "For now, just enjoy your taters!" All the farmers turn back to their conversations.

We start to eat, but Moxie lowers her fork and clears her throat. "We should help these people," she says.

I choke on my chocolate milk. I feel a paralyzing tightness take hold of me. The same tightness I felt when that harpy grabbed Pan. The same feeling I felt as I stood there doing nothing while Moxie and Pan fought off the slithering wormer. It's the feeling that I've gotten us in over our heads.

"I think we should stay focused," I suggest. "Sneak in, get the llama gas, and get out. Let's just do what we came here to do."

"We're going there anyway," says Pan.

"Pan's right," cries Moxie. "Kevin said ogres were guarding the llama. This Tim and Steve is probably their boss. We'll just take care of him while we're there."

"Look, it sounds super exciting," I say. "Really. But this two-headed thing sounds like big trouble."

Moxie slaps Buzzlock's book on the table. "It's probably an ettin." She flips through the pages. "Water Weirdo . . . Lamia . . . Kobold . . . here we go—Ettin!"

ETTIN

Enormous two-headed humanoid creature.

Often becomes chieftain over tribes of dumber creatures like trolls or ogres.

Hard to sneak up on. One eye always open.

Much bigger than an ogre and double the ugly.

Moxie looks up. "It's big, but not as big as a slithering wormer. I bet we can handle it."

Maybe it's just me who's in over my head. A vision swims in my mind. Worse than Pan getting eaten by a harpy. Worse than Moxie getting mauled by an owlbear. It's a vision of Pan and Moxie realizing that this average wannabe mage is holding them back. And they leave me behind.

I shake the thought away and point at the picture on the page. "Two heads! Bigger than an ogre! Have either of you ever fought an ettin?"

"No," Pan says, crossing her arms. "But a week ago I'd never fought a hobgoblin either."

"Or a harpy," says Moxie. "Plus, there's a reward!"

"Yeah, but..."

"This is not about the reward," says Pan. She stares at me pointedly. "I thought you wanted to be a hero."

I shove a big hero-size bite of tater in my mouth and chew it. Heroically. "I do."

"Well, this is what heroes do," she says. "They help people who can't help themselves."

Sheesh. What am I supposed to say to that?

"We're doing it," she says.

I glare at her. "Who made you the leader of our group?"

"Nobody," she says quietly. "It's just who I am."

Pan stands up. "Listen closely, fair people. We are traveling to the Caves of Catastrophe. We are slaying Tim and Steve. And we shall return to you triumphant."

A stillness settles over the room. Then . . .

The villagers turn back to their drinks, excitedly naming all the horrifying creatures that will bring us to our grisly end.

I turn to Pan. "A banshee?" I cry. "THE ROTTING OOZE?"

"Relax," she says calmly. "I'm sure they're exaggerating."

I think we're in serious trouble. I don't say it out loud. But I can feel it. Deep down in my taters.

CHAPTER FIFTEEN

Something tells me it's going to take more than just presentation to survive this.

I stay up late studying Master Elmore's spellbook. I work on my new spell. I try to learn some others, but I'm terrified to find that I can't understand much of what's written on the pages.

I'm starting to realize that Master Elmore wasn't just a cranky old coot. He was a really powerful wizard. And now I've lost him.

What if I can't figure this out? What if Pan's right? What if I'm just a joke?

I don't sleep well that night. But, well rested or not,

we suit up at first light and head into the super-spooky Foothills of Bumble.

An hour into our morning hike, the trees all turn into evergreens and the ground starts to slope sharply uphill. The air fills with a deep buzzing noise. Moxie grips her hammer nervously. Pan holds her bo staff at the ready. I try to look ominous. Then I catch sight of the source of the buzzing.

"Stay calm," says Pan. "It's only giant bees."

"Hear that, Moxie?" I cry. "It's only GIANT BEES!"

"They won't hurt you if you leave them alone," Pan says. She stops suddenly and looks back the way we came.

"What's wrong?" asks Moxie.

"Nothing," says Pan, shaking her head. "Let's keep going."

We keep climbing uphill. We catch glimpses of hives and bee clusters here and there, but Pan is right. They just go on with their busy bee work and don't seem to notice us. Pan keeps acting edgy, stopping and listening every now and again.

About an hour later, we stumble upon an old, abandoned farm cart.

"Let's stop here and rest," I say. "My feet hurt."

Pan is staring behind us. Listening.

"You keep doing that," I say.

"Doing what?" she asks, distracted.

"Looking behind us. What's the problem?"

"Stay here," she says. "I'll be right back." She springs up the nearest tree like some agile pointy-eared squirrel. I see her leap to another tree and then she's gone.

Moxie pulls out her war hammer and paces around the wreckage of the cart. "Something bad happened here," she says. She reaches behind the cart and lifts a massive spear as thick as my arm.

"This is an ogre-size spear," says Moxie.

I feel my stomach drop. "That's an ettin-size spear," I say.

Moxie drops it and looks around nervously. "We must be close to the caves," she says. "Which is the perfect time for our monk to abandon us."

Bzzz

A weird
lump rises
in my throat. "You don't honestly think
she'd leave us, do you?"

"No, I'm just joking." Moxie grins.
"She wouldn't do that."

"I don't know," I say.

"I think she's kinda funny," says Moxie. "Once you give her a chance."

"Funny?" I laugh. "I'm not even sure she has a sense of humor."

We hear a thump. Then a squeak. Moxie turns, hammer raised. I get ready to cast a spell, in case we need to do something, like . . . I dunno . . . talk to a bird. Or make a cozy fire. Or any of the other super-useful things I can do with magic.

A shadow trudges through the trees toward us. As it approaches the cart wreckage, we see that it's Pan. She's dragging something behind her.

"Where'd you go?" Moxie asks.

"I heard something," she says.

"What did you hear?" I ask. "A chipmunk?"

"Nope," she says. "A frog."

"*Squeglich pdurfrap*," TickTock mutters in Phiblish.

"Ribbetty-ribbit to you too," says
Pan.

Moxie busts out laughing. She nudges me with her elbow.

"See?" she says, still giggling. "Funny."

CHAPTER SIXTEEN

Questioning a phibling is not a fun way to spend an afternoon. Just so you know.

"Why are you following us, TickTock?" Moxie asks, gripping her hammer tightly.

"You're here to assassinate us, aren't you?" I cry, pointing my most menacing finger in his face. "But we captured you!"

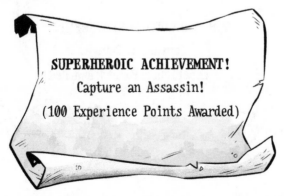

SUPERHEROIC ACHIEVEMENT!
Capture an Assassin!
(100 Experience Points Awarded)

"Never an assassin!" cries the phibling. "Ticktock worries for you!"

"Come on, now," says Moxie. "You wouldn't follow us all the way here just because you were worried about us."

"If you're not an assassin, you're a spy!" I cry.

SUPERHEROIC ACHIEVEMENT!
Capture an Assassin!
(100 Experience Points Awarded)

SUPERHEROIC ACHIEVEMENT!
Capture a Spy!
(100 Experience Points Awarded)

"TickTock is never a spy!" says TickTock.

We're getting nowhere with this guy.

Pan shoves a pointy finger at Moxie and me. "You two. Take it down about seven notches." She kneels calmly next to the phibling. "Look, TickTock. We're not mad . . ."

"Hammer-girl is mad," says TickTock. "And Fart-boy is mad!"

"It's Moxie," says Moxie. "Not Hammer-girl."

"It's Bartok," I say. "Not Fart-boy."

"Whatever!" he says. "And elf-girl threw a ropey thingy at TickTock!"

"It's a bola," Pan says. "Not a ropey thingy."

BOLA

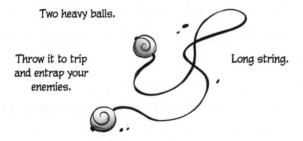

Two heavy balls.

Throw it to trip and entrap your enemies.

Long string.

Never referred to as a "ropey thingy."

Pan sighs. "Look, I didn't know it was you. I heard something following us."

"Now you know it is TickTock," he says. "But Tick-Tock is still tied up."

"We just don't know why you were following us, that's all," says Moxie.

I step toward him. "Maybe you were trying to steal from us."

"Steal what?" he asks. "You got lotsa moneys?"

"No, we don't got lotsa moneys," I say defensively. "But we have other cool stuff, okay?"

"Like what?" asks the phibling.

"Stuff!" I say importantly.

TickTock huffs impatiently. "Not doing stealing!"

"I believe you, TickTock," says Pan. "But we still need to know why you followed us."

TickTock sighs. He looks at the ground thoughtfully. Then he nods. "Untie," he says. "Untie TickTock, and he will speak why."

I look at the other two, unsure.

But Pan reaches down and unwraps the bola. I'm poised for action, in case he tries to take off. But the froggy little guy just sits down on the edge of the cart.

The Great and Powerful Kevin asks TickTock to follow.

"What?" I'm so confused. "Why would Kevin send you to follow us?"

"Him says you are little babies," says TickTock nervously. "He is thinking you will not get out of the caves alive."

"Babies?" says Moxie. "Aw, man! I knew we weren't fooling anyone with these outfits!"

Pan tugs at her hair. "That doesn't explain why he sent you to follow us."

"He is thinking you will be dying from ogres," says TickTock. "He is thinking you will never be coming back. But just in case you are getting the golden gas before you are dying, TickTock will follow you to bring back the golden gas."

"Wait a minute," I say. "You're supposed to follow us, watch us get the golden gas . . ."

"Watch us DIE," says Moxie.

"And then take the golden gas from our cold, dead bodies and return it to Kevin?"

"Yep." TickTock smiles and nods. "That is TickTock's job. If TickTock does it well, Kevin may, at long last, be giving TickTock a title of his own. AND . . . businesss cards!"

I shoot the phibling some side-eye. "Business cards?"

TickTock nods dreamily. "It is TickTock's greatest desire."

Moxie crosses her arms. "Well, if we're supposed to die getting the llama's golden gas, what about you?"

The phibling smiles. "TickTock does not do dying. TickTock is not fighter, but TickTock does sneaking and hiding really good. Nobody is seeing a phibling if a phibling is not wanting them to see. Only if elf ears are hearing."

Pan sits on the cart next to the phibling. "Why does Kevin want this golden gas so badly?"

"Don't know," he says. "It is an ingredient for some magic thing he makes. And he is paying heroes nice if heroes are getting this."

"Wait," says Moxie. "Did you just call us heroes?"

"Uh-huh," says TickTock, nodding. "Baby heroes is

still heroes. Especially baby heroes who take on big, scary quest."

"I like this frog," says Moxie. "I've always said so."

Suddenly, a loud ruckus erupts from the woods nearby.

Moxie grabs her hammer and barrels into the brush. "Come on," she says.

Run toward the scary ruckus sounds? Sure, why not? Pan and I follow with TickTock.

We find Moxie crouching behind some bushes. That's when we see them. A mob of little creatures. They look like . . .

"Hoglings in the foothills," Pan whispers. "Remember what they said in Taterhaven?"

"I hate it when the villagers are right," I say.

"Those aren't hogs," whispers Moxie. "I think they're called snoutkins. No . . . gruntniks. No . . . tuskins! That's it! They're tuskins."

There are more than a dozen of these little pig-guys running around the clearing. They've pulled part of a tree down and they're stabbing big yellow lumps on the ground.

"Aw!" says Moxie. "They're so dang cute! I just want to gather them all up and put them in a basket!"

I shake my head. This girl. "What are they doing?"

"They're killing the bees," says Pan.

She's right. The lumps are dead bees. The buzzing noise has completely disappeared. The tuskins go over to the tree trunk and start packing something into a large wooden chest.

They close the chest and lock it tight. It takes six of the little guys to lift it, but they hoist it up and turn.

Right toward us.

We lock eyes with them. They start snorting nervously, and gently put down the chest.

"Well, I really hate clobbering cute things," says Moxie. She stands up from behind the bush and pulls her shield onto her arm. "But it's time to see if the frog is right. It's time to find out if baby heroes are still heroes."

"I'm still not sure I trust the frog," I say. I turn to the phibling. "Look, TickTock, you wait here, and . . ."

But TickTock is gone.

CHAPTER SEVENTEEN

That sneaky little toad has taken off, but the tuskins are still there. And they may be adorable, but they mean business.

Three of them shoot arrows our way.

THUNK! THUNK! THUNK! Moxie catches them in her shield.

Moxie does what she does best. Besides burping, I mean. She charges in, hammer swinging. She's taken out two of them before they know what hit them. The rest raise their spears and attack.

Pan leaves my side and launches herself into the fray, bo staff flying.

I can feel my heart pounding through my chest. I grip

my staff tightly. I refuse to be helpless. I refuse to be use-less. When one gets too close, I give it a conk, sending it sprawling to the ground. I feel something near my feet and end up beating a small bush senseless.

Moxie has whacked down two more. Pan is surrounded by three of them. She holds them at bay with her quick stickwork, but they keep whacking her in the ankles with their little spears. Suddenly her staff twirls like a blur, and all three tuskins crumple to the ground around her.

Eight remain. They stand back, guarding the wooden chest, but seeing that they are the last line of defense, they pull out small swords and prepare to charge.

"Gets 'em!" one snorts.

SHWICK!

My eye catches a blur of movement through the air, and suddenly one of the tuskins is trapped against the chest by some sort of sticky net.

SHWICK! SHWICK!

Two more tuskins find themselves spider-wrapped to the chest.

I remember the villagers saying something about spider-bats, and I feel a shiver go down my spine. That's all we need at this moment. Enormous flying creepy-crawlies.

Pan and Moxie hold their positions, staring at the

last tuskins. Twenty feet away, the tuskins stare back uncertainly. Then I hear it.

Clank! Clank! Clank!

Out from the trees rolls a little mechanical toy.

Clank! Clank! Clank!

It rolls right to the middle of the clearing. The tuskins look at Moxie and Pan, expecting a trap of some sort. But our expressions mirror their own . . . complete confusion.

The five tuskins approach the wind-up dragon cautiously. It is a stunning creation . . . even these mud-munchers can see this.

Clank! Clank! Clank!

The lead tuskin bends down and picks it up. "Mine!" it squeals. The dragon continues to clank in the tuskin's hand. He closes his palm around it and starts to put it in his pocket, and that's when . . .

KA-BLAMMO!

The little dragon explodes in a ball of smoke.

Moxie dives behind her shield. Pan hits the dirt. I just stand there, mouth hanging open.

When the smoke clears, the last five tuskins are toast.

"Always works," says a voice. "Every time."

TickTock emerges from the trees.

I can't believe it.

"TickTock?" I ask. "You didn't take off?"

He slaps his hand over his face. "Taking off? And leave you to fight these piggie-things? TickTock is not taking off. Told you. TickTock is helpful."

SUPERHEROIC ACHIEVEMENT!
Capture a Spy!
(100 Experience Points Awarded)

SUPERHEROIC ACHIEVEMENT!
Make a Friend!
(250 Experience Points Awarded)

He picks up a little metal wing. It's all that's left of the exploding dragon. "So sad," he murmurs. "It is taking TickTock so long to make, and then boom!"

He looks up at us. "But when dragon is so pretty, bad guys always pick it up. Every time." He grins.

Moxie turns a huge half-moon smile to us. "Can we keep him?"

CHAPTER EIGHTEEN

Moxie yanks the three web-wrapped tuskins free from the chest and ties them to a nearby tree.

The webby stuff that holds them is sticky like taffy.

"TickTock's invention." He pulls up his sleeve to reveal a mini crossbow attached to his arm. "TickTock calls it 'Webbed Fingers.' Get it? Cuz frogs have webbed fingers and TickTock is kind of being like a frog?"

"But not one," Moxie points out.

"But not one!" says TickTock, smiling. "Hammer-girl is catching on! Hammer-girl is smarter than she is looking!"

Pan squeezes TickTock's arm. "Thank you, TickTock."

TICKTOCK'S "WEBBED FINGERS"

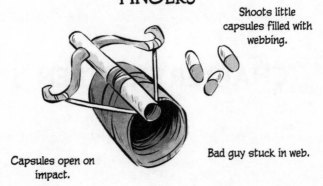

Shoots little capsules filled with webbing.

Capsules open on impact.

Bad guy stuck in web.

"Yeah," I chime in. "You saved our butts."

"Told you," he says. "TickTock worries for you. Tick-Tock is not a hero, but he does sneaking and hiding real good."

"Well, there's no shame in hiding." Moxie sidles up to the wooden chest. "Speaking of hiding, let's see what goodies are hiding in here." She grabs for the lid.

"STOP!" says TickTock, slapping her hand away. "A hero is never just opening a bad-guy chest. Always checking first!"

"OW!" yells Moxie, rubbing her fingers. "Bad phibling! We do not hit!"

He kneels before the chest. Reaching into his belt,

he pulls out a tube with dials and gears all over it. TickTock places one end up to the padlock and peeks through the other end. He fiddles with gears. He turns dials.

Click. He holds up his gizmo and inspects it. A tiny metal claw at the tip holds something thin and shiny.

A needle.

"Just what TickTock is thinking," he says, holding the needle out to us. "Poison needle."

"Poison?" Moxie gulps.

"Yep! Hammer-girl opens this chest with having no key, with having no TickTock, Hammer-girl is dead from poison in thirty seconds."

Moxie sits down hard on the ground. Her hands grip and ungrip the handle of her hammer anxiously. "Whoa," she says.

TickTock pats her on the back. "Not worrying, Hammer-girl. TickTock is here."

She looks up at the phibling. "Sorry I yelled at you, TickTock. You feel free to slap my hand anytime you want. You're a good friend."

"Wait," says TickTock. He looks confused. "Hammer-girl calls TickTock friend?"

"Big time," she says. "Why? What's wrong?"

TickTock shakes his little blue head. His eyes shine with tears. "It is just . . . ever since TickTock is a tadpole, nobody ever says 'friend' to TickTock."

"What?" asks Pan. "Never?"

"No," says the phibling wistfully. "Phiblings call TickTock weirdo. And muckbrains. And gearhead. Even Kevin calls TickTock lackey and flunky! But nobody is calling TickTock friend."

Moxie grips his hand. "Well, I do."

"So do I," says Pan.

I clear my throat. "Me too. Now can we open this chest?"

"Fart's right," says Moxie, dashing over to the chest. "I bet there's some sweet treasure in here!"

She lifts the lid. It's not a pile of gold. It's not oodles of rubies. It's not a magical dragon-slaying sword of power. It's . . .

Goop. Several big jars filled with some sort of golden goop.

"Ooooh," I say excitedly. "Golden goop! I bet it's a potion!" My potions lessons with Master Elmore start scrolling through my head. "Maybe it's a potion of invisibility. Those are yellow. Maybe it's . . . AAH!"

She smirks. "That's good, then. Because it's not a potion." She musses my hair with her gooey fingers. "It's honey."

"But you didn't know that!"

"Of course I did," she says calmly. "The tuskins killed the bees and pulled down their hives. They filled some jars with a yellow syrupy liquid. It's obviously honey."

TickTock nods. "Yep. Piggies are doing stealing because honey is yummy."

"See? TickTock gets it," Pan says to me. "It's basic logic."

Moxie grins and picks at my gooey bangs. "It also works pretty good as hair gel."

"Well, that's pretty rotten treasure, if you ask me."

"Hey, I agree!" says Moxie. "Look around. I bet these tuskins have some other treasure."

They spread out and begin searching. I try to wipe the honey out of my hair with the end of my robes.

And then I hear it. Buzzing.

About fifty feet away, one of the giant bees stumbles onto its legs. It's woozy. But it's still giant. It's still a bee. And it looks seriously cheesed-off at being stabbed and left for dead.

Its bee-sniffer quickly realizes that I have a head full

of honey. It wiggles its stinger-tipped heinie, shakes its head angrily, and zooms straight at me.

"Fart!" yells Moxie, from all the way across the clearing. She's too far to help, but Moxie is a girl of action. She flings her war hammer through the air.

It misses by a mile. It misses *the bee* by a mile. It whacks into a tree trunk a foot from my head.

Sheesh.

TickTock shoots one of his net capsules. He's too far away. It hits the ground, trapping some menacing tufts of grass.

Pan flings her bola, but the bee dips and bobs. The bola wraps tightly around my knees. Stupid ropey thingy.

An angry bee the size of a baby elephant is shooting toward me. I'm about to be shish-kebabed on a stinger the size of a scimitar and all I can do is stand there. Helpless. Useless. Worthless.

"Fart!" Pan cries. "Your new spell!"

There's no time.

The bee will be on me in seconds.

I close my eyes and wait for death by bumblebee.

"You can do this," whispers Pan. "I trust you."

In that moment, clarity comes. The magical gestures form in my mind, and I feel my hands doing them. The words scroll across my brain, and I hear my mouth speaking them, just like I practiced: "*Pepper-puppy-papyrus!*"

I feel the weight of the bee hit me. I'm knocked to the ground. I wait to be skewered by an enormous stinger.

It doesn't come. Instead, I feel something sloppy and wet coating my face.

I peel an eye open.

It's the giant bee. Licking me. With its long, slobbery bee tongue.

I'm alive. And juicy.

Moxie rushes over, daggers drawn. "Hold on, Fart! I'll save you!"

I hold up a hand. "Wait! I think it's okay."

"Fart-boy's spell did the trick!" says TickTock. "Stopped the bee from doing attack. What is this spell called?"

The bee hops off my chest as the others approach. It crouches down and . . . wags its stinger? Yep, that's what it's doing. It's acting just like a . . .

Puppy. "It's called Puppy Power. It's supposed to turn my enemy into a puppy."

The bee runs around us, panting. It grabs a mouthful of my robes and pulls at them, growling playfully.

Pan smirks. "I think you did it wrong."

"Yeah," I say. "No doi."

"You said Pepper-puppy-PAPPY-rus," she points out. "That word is pronounced 'pa-PIE-russ'."

"Thank you for the phonics lesson, Pan."

"How long is this bee going to think it's a puppy?" she asks critically.

"I'm not sure." I grin. "Wanna play fetch?" I ask the bee, waving the stick in the air. I chuck the stick into the trees. The bee beats its wings ferociously and zips after it.

"Awww!" cries Moxie. "Look at its little bumbly butt go! It's so cute!"

The bee comes buzzing back. It drops the stick at my feet and wags its stinger excitedly.

I bend down and pet its fuzzy, bulbous back. It immediately rolls over, showing me its striped belly. I rub it vigorously. "Who's a good bee? Who is? WHO IS?"

Moxie looks at Pan. "Can we keep her? Huh? Can we?"

I turn to Pan with puppy-dog eyes. "Yeah, Pan! Come on! I'll feed her every day! I promise!"

The bee seems to understand what's at stake. She flutters up to Pan and licks her face with that long nectar-gathering tongue.

Pan wipes bee spit from her face. "I don't see how we have a choice," she says. "She's not going anywhere."

SUPERHEROIC ACHIEVEMENT!
Gain a Weird Animal Companion!
(100 Experience Points Awarded)

I rub the bee's fuzzy face. "I'm going to name you Bizzy."

"Awwww!" says Moxie. "'Cuz she's a bee!"

Pan looks across the clearing. "Did you find any treasure?" she asks Moxie.

Moxie lets out a frustrated sigh. "Nope," she says. "It's weird. Not a single silver piece."

Pan nods her head. "Undoubtedly, these tuskins are just servants."

"Servants?" asks Moxie. "To who?"

"HURRY UP WITH THAT HONEY, YOU SQUEALING OINKERS! WE AIN'T GOT ALL DAY!"

We hit the dirt. I belly crawl to the bushes and peek through. I feel Pan, Moxie, TickTock, and Bizzy creep up beside me. There, through the trees, I glimpse it. A cavern, yawning open like the mouth of some horrible monster that wants to gobble us all up.

LET'S GO, PORKINS!

"Servants to them," hisses Pan.

TickTock lets out a gasp. "Ogres."

I feel a sinking feeling in the pit of my stomach, like I'll never see another butterfly or birthday cake ever again. Which might be true.

Because we've just found the Caves of Catastrophe.

CHAPTER NINETEEN

"I want it on the record," I whine at Pan. "I hate this plan of yours." The helmet keeps falling over my eyes. And the rags I'm wearing reek. Not in the good way. "These clothes smell like piglet heinie."

"Your objections have been noted," says Pan. "However, I'm too tall to pass for a tuskin. So it has to be you and Moxie."

Moxie elbows me. "I think she's calling us short."

"Don't let anything happen to Bizzy," I tell Pan.

"Don't worry," Pan assures me. "We'll be watching you the whole time. As soon as the coast is clear, we'll join you. Unless you die. Then we'll leave and never come back."

True friendship. It makes me want to weep. Not in the good way.

Moxie and I hoist the heavy chest and trudge toward the cave.

"HURRY UP, YOU TROTTERS! OR SLAGGO MAKE BARBECUE OUT OF YOU!" The ogres are getting impatient. I can tell because the death threats are getting louder.

Moxie and I waddle out of the trees, doing our best tuskin shuffle toward the cave.

"About time!" growls one of the ogres. Gosh, they're big up close. Like, mountain big. Like, nightmare big.

"Hey! Slaggo!" says one, waving a board with nails sticking out of it.

"What you want, Mobo?" says the other one.

Mobo scratches her giant ham head. "How many porkins go get honey in woods?"

"I dunno," shrugs Slaggo. "You know numbers make Slaggo's head hurt. Why you ask?"

"Well, me can count to two." Mobo itches her nose ring and points to us. "Two porkins. One. Two. Like that."

"Yeah, yeah," says Slaggo. "That why you gatekeeper. Can do puzzle. Gotta count to do puzzle."

Mobo scratches her head. She's trying hard to work it out.

"Me think more than two go into woods to get honey," she finally says. "But only two come back."

Slaggo turns back to us. "Wait a second. Slaggo check." He points to Moxie. "One . . ." He points to me.

Silence.

More silence.

Still more silence.

"Two," whispers Mobo.

"ME KNOW HOW TO DO IT! TWO!" Slaggo shakes his club at us. "Where other porkins?"

We drop the chest before them and fall to our knees, groveling. "All dead!" Moxie squeals.

It's not bad, as tuskin impressions go.

"All dead?" asks Slaggo. "How?"

"Bees do it," squeaks Moxie. "Stingy stingy! Ow! Ow!"

Mobo nods. "Bees stingy stingy."

"Yeah," Slaggo says, grinning. "That's why porkers go get honey. Not ogres. We smart!"

Mobo scratches her butt. "You get honey?" she asks us.

Moxie nods and pats the chest. "We get! We get!"

"Hey, Slaggo! Maybe we try honey first," she says. "You know. Make sure it good honey. Before we take to the boss."

Slaggo's face cracks into a big, toothless grin. "Smart idea, Mobo!"

"Darn right, smart!" says Mobo proudly. "That why Mobo can count all the way to two!"

"Get out of way, porkers," Slaggo says, shoving us aside. "Need to taste honey." He pulls a key from the folds of his filthy loincloth.

Slaggo and Mobo lean over the chest eagerly.

Click! Slaggo undoes the padlock. He lifts the lid.

SHWICK! SHWICK!

TickTock pops out of the chest. Quicker than a

greased tuskin, he's shot two of his webby wads into the eyes of the ogres.

Moxie has already pulled her hammer from beneath the rags. She gives Mobo a thump to the kneecap. The ogre crumples with a howl of pain.

Pan comes leaping from the trees like a very pointy gazelle. She flings her bola around Slaggo's ankles, wrapping them tight.

I dart toward Slaggo. With a quick whisper, I chant the spell for Cozy Campfire.

Slaggo's clawing at his eyes with one hand and swinging his club with the other. But suddenly he notices the burn in his shag shorts. He bellows and does what anyone would do when they realize their underpants are on fire. He runs.

But his ankles are all bound up, and there's nowhere to go.

TIMBER!!!!

Ogre face, meet solid oak chest. Wood splinters. Bones crack. And it's good night, sweet Slaggo.

I turn to find Moxie has a nasty gash to the arm from Mobo's wildly swinging spike stick.

But that's when TickTock springs into action like some tiny amphibious jaguar. Right onto Mobo's face.

He smacks her again and again. *SMACK! SMACK!* It isn't deadly, but it looks super annoying.

Mobo grips her enormous stick with both hands and swings it—just as TickTock leaps—and wallops herself right in her own noggin.

SMASHEROOSKI!

With the ogres put to bed, I look over the mayhem. "Wow!" I cheer. "Nice job, TickTock!"

"Nice job?" The phibling starts to get misty again. "Kevin only ever says adequate!" He blows his nose on his sleeve.

Moxie suddenly collapses against the rock face. She drops her hammer and presses firmly on her wounded arm.

"Moxie?" I whisper. "Are you okay?"

Moxie grins through gritted teeth. "I'll be fine, magic meathead. Just a cut."

"You're hurt," Pan says, rushing to her side. Bizzy flutters next to us and nuzzles me.

Pan digs into her pack and pulls out a small leaf wrapped around some muddy brown goo.

She smears the glop onto Moxie's arm and whispers a chant. The brown stuff glows with a soft green light.

Moxie's face relaxes. The tension and pain drains away. "Whoa. That's better."

"What did you do?" I ask Pan. She's wrapping a strip of cloth around Moxie's smudge-stained arm.

"Zen healing," says Pan softly. "This mud contains healing minerals. I was able to manipulate the nurturing elements into her wound."

Moxie stands up and flexes her arm. "Yeah, you did! It feels better already!"

I clap slowly. "Sheesh, Pan. That's some sweet monk mojo. Impressive!"

She raises an eyebrow. "I cannot heal completely. Not yet. But I can ease the pain and speed the healing. It should be fully healed in a day or two."

Pan stands and nods at me. "But thank you," she says softly.

Together, we turn slowly toward the cave entrance. A stone arch towers over us. The wind rattles bones that dangle from the opening.

Moxie looks up at the yellow symbol carved at the top. I thought it was a snake. But now that we're closer, I see that it's not, really—it's a snake with a human face. A female human face.

"I wonder what that image means," says Moxie curiously. "It's like a snake lady."

"Look here," says Pan, pointing inside the cave. "There's another one."

Just within the entrance, the cavern dead-ends at a stone wall. Statues loom from the darkness, daring us to come closer. Colored gems sparkle from each statue's mouth: blue, red, yellow, and, at the top, purple.

TWO IS THE KEY
NOT THREE

"The ogre said something about being a gatekeeper," Moxie reminds us.

"There's a gap here," says Pan, running her fingers along the arched crack in the stone. "A secret door."

"Oooh, secret door!" cries TickTock. "Elf-girl got good eyes!"

Moxie kicks at the wall. Nothing. She wallops it with her hammer. Nada.

Moxie huffs. "If this is a door, I think it's broken."

"You won't open it by force," says Pan, studying the wall before us.

"TickTock, can you use your little lock-picking gizmo to open it?" I ask.

He just shrugs. "No keyhole."

"I say we just pry these fat gems out and be done with it," says Moxie, readying her hammer. "That's one sparkly jewel for each of us."

Pan shakes her head. "No. I believe these gems are the key to getting inside. Like a lock."

"You know how to solve it?" I ask.

Pan reaches out to the blue jewel. It glows at her touch. She smirks. "Yes, I think so. And so do you. It's quite simple. Even an ogre can do it." She points to the face carved into the stone. "The creature at the top holds a purple gem. Which of the other gems will get you to the purple gem?"

Moxie scratches her chin. "Umm . . ."

"Two is the key," says Pan. "Not three."

I move forward and press the red gem. It glows brightly. "Red," I say. "Plus blue." I press the blue gem. It also glows. "Equals purple."

The purple gem glows brightly. We hear the sound of stone grinding upon stone.

Moxie laughs. "Easy!" She stares at the carving thoughtfully. "That snake lady thing gives me a weird feeling. Like I've seen it before."

Bizzy nuzzles against me and whimpers.

"It's giving Bizzy a weird feeling too. Like if we keep standing here, more ogres are going to show up and murdalize us." I shrug off the tuskin rags and pull two torches from my backpack. There's a nearby piece of Slaggo's burnt loincloth, still smoldering. I touch the torches to it, and they blaze to life.

"Come on," I say, passing one to Moxie. "We've got a golden llama to find. Glory and riches await."

"Glory and riches," everyone repeats. Moxie grabs the torch and slowly ducks into the cave entrance. Pan and TickTock follow.

I glance behind us. The sunlight is fading over the treetops. Soon, there will be nothing but darkness.

I sigh, scratch Bizzy's head, and plunge into the Caves of Catastrophe.

CHAPTER TWENTY

We enter a rough stone tunnel, about ten feet wide. Bones litter the floor. The path before us slopes slowly downward into the bowels of the hill.

And I do mean bowels. It smells like an outhouse exploded in here.

"Disgusting," Moxie whispers. "These ogres are slobs!"

Our voices echo uncomfortably in the silence.

"Hey," Moxie says, coming to a halt. "Check this out." She lowers her torch to the floor. Set into the stone is a trail of tiny silver tiles. The sparkling trail of tile starts at the cave entrance. They snake down the corridor and into the darkness beyond.

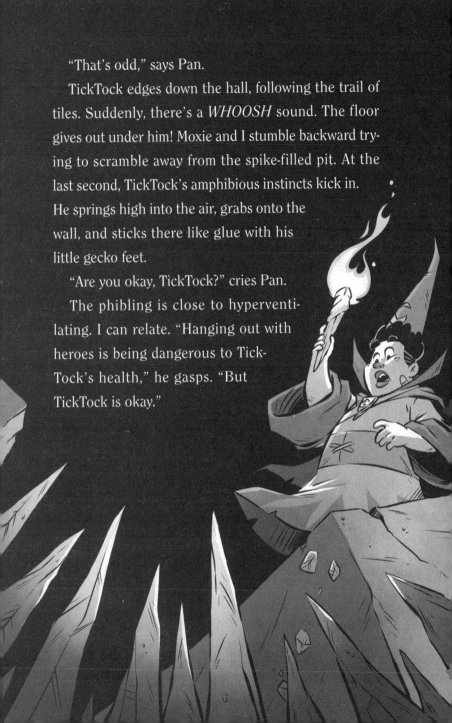

"That's odd," says Pan.

TickTock edges down the hall, following the trail of tiles. Suddenly, there's a *WHOOSH* sound. The floor gives out under him! Moxie and I stumble backward trying to scramble away from the spike-filled pit. At the last second, TickTock's amphibious instincts kick in. He springs high into the air, grabs onto the wall, and sticks there like glue with his little gecko feet.

"Are you okay, TickTock?" cries Pan.

The phibling is close to hyperventilating. I can relate. "Hanging out with heroes is being dangerous to TickTock's health," he gasps. "But TickTock is okay."

"Crud on a cracker," I mutter. I peek down into the pit. "That was too close."

"Don't step feet on the tiles," says TickTock breathlessly. "A pit is opening to stab you dead."

"Good safety tip," says Moxie, dusting herself off.

TickTock hops lightly down from the wall and rejoins us. Moxie picks her torch off the floor, carefully sidesteps the silver tiles, and leads us slowly into the waiting darkness.

Aside from the comforting buzz of Bizzy hovering beside me, it's really quiet. I would say *too quiet*, but somebody always dies right after they say that. So I'm not saying it.

We travel about one hundred feet down the sloping corridor, then it comes to a halt. One path leads to the right. Another goes left.

"The trail of tiles goes left," Moxie points out. "No tiles to the right."

The phibling shudders. "TickTock votes for no tiles."

"I'm with TickTock," says Moxie. "No tiles means no danger, if you ask me."

I look to the trail of tiles. They sparkle tantalizingly in the darkness. "Unless it's a trick," I say.

"Explain," says Pan.

I turn to her. "Remember the harpy on the road? She looked innocent, but it was a trick. She was actually super dangerous."

Pan nods. "Keep going."

"So maybe the pit full of spikes is designed to make us think following the tiles is dangerous. To get us to avoid the tiles. Maybe the tiles actually lead to the good stuff. Maybe the tiles lead to the golden llama."

Moxie shakes her head. "Nope. Very bad idea."

But Pan looks pleased with me. "Fart, that is impressively logical."

"Well, don't ruin it by calling me logical," I mutter. But deep inside, I know that's her elfy way of saying my idea is brilliant. Which feels pretty good, I'm not going to lie.

"Pan," says Moxie. "I really don't think we should—"

But Pan cuts her off. "We'll follow the tiles. For now."

TickTock turns to Moxie. "We all gonna die," he whimpers.

Moxie shakes her head. She sighs loudly. But she shines her torchlight down the corridor to the left and leads the way into the blackness before us.

It's not long, maybe five or ten minutes, before I can make out a soft glow. The glint of something shiny coming from the hallway ahead.

"What is that?" I wonder aloud.

As we approach, our torches reveal exactly what it is. A giant snake head.

"Why is the head glowing like that?" I ask.

"It is not doing a glow, Fart-boy," says TickTock.

I clearly see a blue glow around it. And then it hits me. My ring!

"It's glowing with magic!" I say. "This whole head is some type of magical thing."

"Good magic?" asks Moxie. "Or bad magic?

"I can't tell."

"The hallway continues into the mouth," says Pan. "This is clearly a doorway of some kind."

"A magical doorway," I remind her.

And then I hear it. The voice. Echoing softly from the darkness beyond the snake head. "Bartok . . . don't leave me . . ."

My heart stops. I can't believe it. It's the voice of my dad. *Don't leave me*. Those are the same words I said to him when he brought me to Krakentop. The last words I ever spoke to him.

I take a step toward the mouth. "Did you hear that voice?"

Moxie has turned white as a ghost. "Yes! It's Master Redmane!"

"No it's not! It's my dad!"

"Wrong!" cries the phibling. "Tick-Tock is hearing Kevin calling!"

"You are all incorrect," says

Pan, creeping closer to the mouth. "That is the voice of my mother."

"You guys, let's go!" Moxie cries, stepping toward the opening. "Master Redmane is alive! He needs me!"

"Stop!" Pan swings her bo staff out to block Moxie.

"Hey!" Moxie roars.

"I apologize, Moxie. But I had to stop you." Pan levels her gaze at the dwarf. "Did you say you hear Master Redmane?"

"Yes!" cries Moxie, rising to her feet.

"And I hear my mother." Pan crosses her arms. "Both Master Redmane and my mother are dead." A steely look comes into her eyes. "This is not logical. Or possible."

Her voice penetrates my brain, drowning out the soft voice of my dad.

"You're wasting time!" Moxie cries angrily, moving toward the mouth. "Maybe Master Redmane survived. He needs me! Besides, I thought we decided the tiles were good now!"

The sparkling tiles lead right into the mouth of the snake and into the darkness beyond. And as I look closer now, I see that the tiles themselves sparkle with a glimmer of blue. The aura of magic! Luring us into following them!

Pan eyes the snake head skeptically. "This is clearly another trap of some sort."

"Yeah," TickTock chimes in. "No way the Great and Powerful Kevin is down that spooky hallway. Kevin is not coming here. Kevin is sending TickTock!" He wrings his hands together. "TickTock got a bad feeling about this mouth."

Pan nods. "Good thinking, TickTock."

Moxie huffs in frustration. "How come nobody ever says 'Good thinking, Moxie'?"

"Moxie, I—" Pan begins.

"I say, 'Let's take the gems from the snake statues.' Wrong answer! I say, 'Let's not follow the tiles.' Wrong answer!" Moxie grips and ungrips her hammer angrily. "I'm not just the dumb muscle around here, you know!"

"Moxie," I start. "We don't think—"

"And I say Master Redmane needs me!"

Pan sets her jaw firmly. "That is not Master Redmane."

"It's a trick!" I tell her. "The voice. The tiles. They're magic! They're trying to lure us in there!"

But she's not listening.

"Here, I'll prove it's okay!" says Moxie, grabbing a bone from the floor. "I'll throw this into the mouth." She waves the bone in the air. "I'll prove that nothing bad is going to happen. Then we can quit arguing and go save Master Redmane!"

Moxie twirls the bone through the air and hurls it into the snake mouth.

Only in that moment do I realize that Bizzy has been eyeballing the bone this whole time, stinger wagging, ready to play fetch. Bizzy leaps forward, wings flapping, to snatch the bone from midair.

When I open my eyes, both the bone and Bizzy have been zapped into oblivion.

"BIZZY!" I cry.

I run to the edge of the mouth. The trail of silver tiles still disappears into the darkness. But Bizzy . . . is gone.

Pan reaches out and places her hand on my shoulder. "I think I know what kind of magic this doorway is."

"Bad magic," I snarl. "Really bad magic."

CHAPTER TWENTY-ONE

The sizzling of Bizzy seems to break the spell over Moxie.

She looks horror-struck. "Oh my gosh!"

TickTock holds his head in his hands. "TickTock knew it!"

Moxie reaches out for us. "Fart . . . Pan . . . I . . ." Her voice fades. Her eyes focus on me, like she's waking up from a bad dream. "I'm so sorry. That is all my fault."

I pull away. "You think?!"

"I didn't mean for that to happen!" Her eyes well up with tears.

Even in my anger, it hits me. In all the danger we've faced since we left Krakentop, I've only seen Moxie cry once before. When Master Redmane died. She gets whacked by a hobgoblin's club? Not a whimper. Slashed by an ogre's spike stick? Not a single teardrop.

But now . . .

...she's crying.

"I just . . . It was Master Redmane."

"I know," I say, trying hard to cool off. "I heard my dad calling."

"It was meant to lure us to our doom," Pan says.

Moxie sinks to her knees and wipes her eyes with her tattered cloak. "I'm sorry, you guys. When Master Redmane found me as an orphan, I was all alone. Nobody ever listened to me until he came along. And now that he's gone . . ." She trails off into sniffles.

I feel my anger draining away.

I kneel next to her. "You're not alone, Moxie. You have me. And Pan. And TickTock. And—" I was going to say Bizzy. But I stop myself.

Moxie looks up at me with tears running through her freckles. "I'm so sorry about Bizzy, Fart."

I swallow the lump in my throat.

"You didn't mean to do it," I say gently.

"I'm so sorry I yelled at you, Pan."

"You were not yourself," says Pan. "But it is my fault too. You didn't wish to come this way, and I didn't listen. From now on, we will decide things together."

"Yeah," I say, nodding in agreement. I find myself agreeing with her more and more these days. It's a little scary. But if it hadn't been for her, we all would have gone charging into that snake head. I don't know if she has some elfy magic resistance or it's just her refusal to believe anything that isn't logical, but she saved us all.

I pull Moxie to her feet. "I think we can all agree that we're definitely not going into the snake head."

Moxie grabs my shoulder. "I think you're right." She shoots me a tentative smile. "Thanks, Fart."

I give her a playful punch in her bandaged shoulder. "You keep forgetting. My name is Bartok the Brilliant."

She manages to wince in pain and grin at the same time. "Okay, Bartok." She wipes her face and picks up her hammer. "Should we head back to the other hallway?"

"Dang right," I say with determination. "We've got ogres to slay."

"I thought the plan was to sneak through this place," says Pan. "Get out before anyone knew we were here."

I grit my teeth. "That was before we had a bee to avenge."

Moxie throws her hand into the middle of our circle. "Agreed."

I put my hand in. "Agreed."

Pan places her hand on mine. "Agreed."

TickTock reaches up and puts his little hand on Pan's. "Friendship is beautiful!" The little guy is blubbering.

Moxie leads us back the way we came.

We return to the split in the hallway. This time, we take the other passage, leaving the tiles behind us.

"Servants' quarters," says Pan. "I bet this is where the tuskins sleep."

After several long minutes, the corridor stops. To the right, a passage runs steadily down. To the left, stairs lead up.

Pan sniffs the air. "So, do we go down, where it smells? Or up, where it smells?"

I step into the right-hand passage. In the distance, *drip-drip-drip* sounds echo off the stone.

"I say down. The deeper you go in the dungeon, the better the treasure. Everybody knows that. If this golden llama is their big treasure, it would be down. Right?"

Moxie nods. Pan nods. TickTock nods. The nods have it. Hey, this teamwork thing really works! A surge of confidence floods

through me. We creep together into the darkness of the right-hand corridor.

Moxie steps protectively into the lead, her torch lighting the way. The walls drip with moisture. The floor is slick. Down, down, down we go.

And then we see it . . . About thirty feet ahead of us, the passage ends. In its place is an underground pool. It fills the large cavern before us.

But something is strange. And then I realize what. No bones. No cobwebs. It's as if the corridor has been scoured clean. And lying on the ground between us and the pool . . .

Moxie turns to me. "I think my eyes are playing tricks on me."

Pan shakes her head. "They are not."

"So," Moxie confirms, "you see the twinkle-twinkle of big fat gemstones lying on the ground?"

"I do indeed," says Pan. "Those look like diamonds."

Something doesn't feel right.

I scan the cavern. The pool. The glistening walls. Blobs of slime glop down the walls like boogers.

Boogers? My mind goes back to Krakentop, to Master Elmore's study. A lesson on the value of a mage in a group of adventurers.

Magic isn't just about casting fireballs! You should be observing what the others are not!

Oh.

For example, there is a particular species of creature that clings to ceilings and drops down on unsuspecting victims, dissolving them instantly with their acid. Warriors never remember to look up.

Looks like a bunch of boogers.

Yes, you ignoramus.

But the proper name for it is the rotting...

"Well!" says Moxie, yanking me out of my thoughts. "Let's not let that treasure go to waste!" She steps forward to claim the gems.

And then I see it.

I slam my staff out, knocking Moxie backward. She tumbles into Pan and they fall to the floor in a knot of armor and robes.

"Hey!" Moxie groans. "What gives?"

There on the ceiling, above the coins, above the rubies, above the lustrous, sparkling diamonds, something looms. There are bones. And a large ogre skull. Stuck to the ceiling.

"Sorry," I say quietly. A shiver runs through my body. "I was saving your life."

"From what?" asks Moxie, standing and pulling Pan to her feet.

I point at the ceiling. "From that." I raise my torch into the air.

"What's the big deal?" says Moxie. "It's just some bones! This place is full of them!"

Pan reaches out to grab Moxie's arm. "Stuck to the ceiling?"

TickTock whispers ominously. "Not just bones."

"TickTock's right," I say. "Look closer." I raise my torch higher.

The light glistens off the ceiling. Illuminating what's really there.

"Oh . . . my . . . gosh . . ." sputters Moxie.

They see it now. Stuck to the ceiling. Waiting to fall upon whoever is foolish enough to step forward and claim the gems.

The rotting ooze.

CHAPTER TWENTY-TWO

I start backing away slowly, expecting that horrible Jell-O mold of doom to come flapping down at us any second.

Moxie raises her torch into the darkness beyond the pool. "There's nothing down here but water anyway."

"And whatever horrors live in that pool," mutters Pan.

"Yeah. That," agrees Moxie. "But definitely no llama."

Minutes later, we're back at the fork in the path. I look behind me nervously. I keep expecting jelly arms to reach out and grab me.

"I guess we go up," says Moxie, pointing at the stairs leading the other way.

The other path just rises about seven or eight uneven steps. We take them slowly. The hallway goes on for about thirty feet and takes a sharp turn to the left. As we turn . . .

We hear voices. Lots of them.

We see light. Lots of it.

Pan uses her fire mojo to snuff our torches so we don't give ourselves away.

The voices are gruff. And rowdy.

"Ogres," Moxie whispers.

My ears tell me there are about twenty or thirty ogres in the room before us. I don't like the odds.

"BUCKET! BUCKET, BUCKET! BUCKET!"

The ogres are chanting and laughing. It must be some ogre game apparently involving a bucket.

I look at the phibling. "TickTock, are you as good at sticking to ceilings as you are at sticking to walls?"

The phibling nods. "Yep, TickTock is professional at the ceiling walking. Why is Fart-boy asking?"

"Maybe you could sneak in and see what our options are? They won't notice you if you're on the ceiling."

Moxie nods. "Yeah, that's good. Maybe you'll spot a way to sneak past them."

Pan turns gently to him. "You don't have to, Tick-Tock. You never signed up for all this."

TickTock looks at each of us in turn. Then he nods his blue head. "It okay. TickTock is good at sneaking."

I turn to check the doorway. That's when I slam face-first into ogre chest hair.

I stumble back. He's as surprised as I am. We both stare at each other, speechless.

It's an ogre. But a runt.

He opens his mouth to scream.

But I move faster. I jump at him, spring onto his shoulders, and slap my hand over his mouth.

Yes, I know. Mages are supposed to hide behind our more burly friends and fling our dazzling magic into

the fray. Well, once in a while, you surprise even yourself.

"Mmmph! Mm-mm-mmph!"

Gross. Ogre spit.

He tries to talk. But my slobber-covered hands get in the way.

I yank out my dagger and hold it to the ogre's throat. "One little peep, and you're done for," I whisper menacingly.

The ogre nods.

"Bucket not say nothing," he whimpers.

For my first time being menacing, I've gotta say . . . I menaced the crap out of this guy.

All this has happened in about three nanoseconds. But Moxie's shock wears off, and she pulls out her hammer to bonk the ogre on the noggin.

Pan stops her. "A source of information has just wandered into our arms. Let's not waste it."

"Good idea." Moxie nods.

Moxie and Pan yank the ogre down the steps. We're

far enough away from the doorway now. But in the spill of light, I see that this little ogre looks scared.

Moxie holds her hammer menacingly. "What's your name, brute?"

"B . . . B . . . Bucket," says the ogre.

"Bucket?" asks Moxie. "What kind of weird ogre name is that?"

The ogre shrugs. "Bucket is Bucket's name. Bucket is Bucket's job."

"Job?" asks Pan.

The ogre holds up the two buckets. Filth slops out onto Moxie's shoes. "Empty potty buckets. Bucket's job."

Potty buckets.

The ogre sets his buckets down. "What humies doing here?" he asks. "Humies never come this way. Always go to snake head. Get zapped to big boss and big boss eat."

Moxie looks at Pan. "The ettin," she mutters. She turns back to Bucket, hammer held near his face. "Don't you worry about us. You help us out, we'll let you live."

Bucket holds up his hands. "Bucket want to live. Bucket will help."

Pan steps close, eyeing Bucket's buckets warily. "How many ogres are in that room?"

Bucket looks back toward the light. "In room? About two. Definitely two."

Moxie grits her teeth. "There are more than two ogres in that room!"

Bucket shrinks back. "Not lying!" He counts on his fingers. "Nuthead. Meatball. Saggack. Dagnab. Chutnee. Potmouth. Gobo . . ." He keeps on going, long past when he's run out of fingers.

Moxie cuts him off. "We get it. A lot of very weirdly named ogres."

"Yeah," says Bucket. "Like I say . . . two."

Pan takes over. "When do they leave, Bucket?"

The ogre shakes his head. "Not leave tonight. Not unless something happen."

Pan perks up. "Something like what?"

Bucket shrugs. "Sometimes gnolls come down from mountains. Ugly dog-mutts. Gotta fight them off. Sometime boss send us for taters at village."

Moxie smiles. "If they only leave when something happens, then we make something happen!"

"What do you mean?" I ask.

"It's easy!" she grins. "We send Bucket back into the room. He feeds them some line about something happening, they run to take care of it . . . *BOOM*! No more ogres!"

"Whoa, whoa, whoa!" I say, clutching Bucket's shoulders. "You're going to trust this guy? As soon as we let him go, he'll give us away!"

Bucket shakes his head ferociously. I grab a fistful of back hair to stop from flying off. "Bucket not tell! Promise!"

Pan looks thoughtful. "Fart is right. Somebody has to go with Bucket to make sure he sticks to the story."

Moxie snaps her fingers. "I got it! Fart holds onto Bucket's shoulders and keeps a dagger at his throat. That'll keep him honest while he's lying to those ogres."

"What?" I cry. "Why me?"

"You're already up there," says Moxie. "Look how comfy you look!"

"I am not comfy!" I cry. "It is very lumpy up here. And it stinks."

Bucket turns his head to me. "Humie not smell so great either."

"Hammer-girl got a good idea," TickTock chimes in. "We cover Fart-boy with ogre bearskin. He is holding on around ogre's neck. The other ogres never are seeing him."

Pan steps back and studies me, perched on the runty ogre. "Especially not if they keep their distance."

"Pffft," I chuckle. "And how are we going to make them keep their distance?"

Pan looks at me. And smiles. Actually smiles. It's super creepy.

"Uh-oh," says TickTock. "Elf-girl got an idea."

"I do," she says.

She walks forward and picks up one of the ogre's potty buckets. "And Fart? This idea is right up your alley. In fact, I can honestly say that you're going to love this idea."

CHAPTER TWENTY-THREE

I can honestly say that I hate this idea.

I am hanging on for dear life to Bucket's neck, dagger in hand. I am covered in his smelly old bear pelt. And we have been doused in ogre poop.

Pan's idea.

Some days, I think she's just messing with me.

Bucket runs into the brightly lit room. From my hidey-hole under Bucket's bearskin, I see a huge room. Fire ripples from a cooking pit in the middle. Bearskins line the edges of the room.

Oh, and did I forget to mention? There are about THIRTY LOUD, SMELLY OGRES.

I shudder at the thought of being discovered.

I give Bucket a little poke with the dagger. Just a little reminder to stay on script. But he does it exactly like we rehearsed in the hallway.

"Come quick!" yells Bucket.

The racket screeches to a halt. They look at the little ogre with disdain. I am familiar with this look.

A big ogre stands up from playing some kind of card game. "What wrong, dumb-bucket?" He's coming close, and I'm getting nervous. But then his eyes widen in alarm. He looks Bucket over and backs away, squeezing his nose shut. "What you got all over you, dumb-bucket?!"

Bucket wipes his hands on his soiled furs. "I go to front door to dump potty buckets! I panic and slop caca all over me!"

Stinky Smelly

Several ogres stand now. "Why you panic?"

"Gnolls attack! Kill Mobo and Slaggo! Kill pig-men! Steal honey!"

Some ogres rise. "What??? Gnolls???"

Some ogres grab clubs and spears. "What??? Mobo and Slaggo dead???"

Some ogres look legitimately concerned. "What??? You got caca all over you???"

Bucket jumps up and down, jostling me all over the place. "Hurry!" he cries. "Gnolls run into mountains when they see Bucket! GETTING AWAY!"

This does it. The ogres grab every weapon within reach and charge out the doorway.

The room clears out in a hurry. We follow them down the stairs, but soon their voices fade away.

Moxie, Pan, and TickTock emerge from the side corridor.

"Not too shabby, Bucket," says Moxie, looking impressed.

I hop down from my roost. "You should have seen him!" I say, tucking my dagger away. "He really sold it!"

Bucket is beaming from ear to ear. "That fun!" he says. "Let's do again!"

Pan sits on the bottom step and smiles at the ogre. "Great job, Bucket," she says. "When you wake up, just tell them the gnolls tied you up."

Bucket scratches his head. "Wake up? Bucket not sleepy."

Pan draws a small tube from her belt, puts it to her mouth, and blows into it. A tiny feathered dart flies through the air and sticks right in the ogre's neck. He feels for it with his hand.

"Bucket sleepy," he says. He smiles at Pan and falls over backward.

We lug him into the ogre room. We drag a fur blanket over him. By the time they find him, we'll be long gone. Or dead.

We four-way fist bump and turn around.

There are three ogres watching us from across the room. Well, crap.

I guess when gnolls attack, not every ogre charges into battle. Apparently three stay behind to keep an eye on the fire. How annoyingly responsible of them.

The ogres shake their heads stupidly, like they can't believe what they're seeing. "Humies?" one says, pointing at us.

"Come on, fellas," says Moxie, sliding her shield onto her arm. "*I* am a dwarf."

She points at Pan as she grips her hammer. "*She* is an elf."

She points at TickTock as she strolls casually toward the ogres. "*He* is a phibling. We're not all humies."

"Gee, you right," says one of the ogres. "Sorry about that."

"Apology accepted," she says. And she launches herself at the ogres like a ninja owlbear.

Moxie swings ferociously, but the ogres block her easily with their huge clubs.

Pan whacks one across the face with her bo staff, taking the attention off Moxie. She pokes and prods like lightning, but she's like a buzzing fly to the ogre. He can't quite swat her, but she's not doing much damage either.

197

It doesn't take long before Moxie is starting to pant. Two ogres have encircled her. TickTock leaps onto one of the ogre's shoulders. The ogre doesn't even notice.

The phibling pulls out a grappling hook attached to a long cable. He lowers it down and hooks the ogre's loincloth. With the other end in hand, the phibling leaps over a ceiling beam and lands lightly at my feet.

The ogre yowls in butt-cheek distress. Moxie conks it hard, right on the noodle.

Down it drops. What a way to go . . . death by wedgie.

The other ogre sends Moxie flying against the wall with a two-ton club swing. She crumples in pain. Moxie pulls herself up and shambles back into battle. But with the way she's wincing, something's broken for sure.

Pan has taken a new strategy. She's just dodging swings, letting her ogre wear itself out.

I look around desperately for something helpful. That's when I spot the cooking fire. Bacon sizzles and burns in an oversize frying pan.

I rush to the firepit. "Hey, Moxie!"

"Yeah?"

"Did you order a side of bacon?" I grab the frying pan and fling the hot contents onto the ogre's back. The grease sizzles on bare skin.

"YEEEEEEOWTCCCCCCHHHHHH!"

The grease-splattered ogre turns on me with fury in its eyes. It raises its club to squash me like a bug.

Moxie swings her war hammer with all her might. I whack with that frying pan like there's no tomorrow.

CLANGGGGGG!

The ogre crumples to the ground with burned bacon still stuck to its leg. I don't know if Moxie's hammer or my frying pan did the job, but since I'm the one telling the story, I'm pretty sure it was my frying pan.

One ogre stands, if you can call it standing. He's crouched over, panting from trying to hit Pan. Pan reaches down, grabs the bearskin that he's standing on, and gives it a yank.

It doesn't budge.

"Ha-ha! Nice try, little elf. But Dagnab too big for you!"

Moxie, TickTock, and I walk over to stand next to Pan. We reach down. We grab the bearskin. And we yank.

Dagnab goes flying backward. There's a loud *crack* as he smacks his head against the firepit.

"That move will forever be referred to as Dagnabbing It," I say.

SUPERHEROIC ACHIEVEMENT!
Invent a Clever Catchphrase!
(50 Experience Points Awarded)

Moxie has broken ribs. Pan is breathing hard. Tick-Tock is a pale shade of blue. And I think I burned my thumb on that pan.

What we really need is a nice, long rest with no fighting and no monsters.

"WHAT IS GOING ON IN HERE?!" a horrible voice roars. "THE EARS ON MY ONE HEAD CAN'T HEAR THE MOUTH ON MY OTHER HEAD!"

At the other end of the room, a gigantic oak door has flown open. And standing in the doorway . . . a nightmare from our darkest fever dreams.

It's Tim and Steve.

CHAPTER TWENTY-FOUR

I gulp. I gulp again. I gulp a third time.

"You are way bigger than in your wanted poster," I tell the ettin.

One of the ettin heads grins. Tim, maybe. Or it might be Steve. Not really sure.

"I have a wanted poster?" it says. "How awesome is that?"

"And you're way uglier than in *Buzzlock's Big Book of Beasts*," says Moxie.

The other head sniffs. "Well, now you're just being hurtful."

"It's true," Moxie says, grinning through the pain. "I am."

I look around at our sad group. We are in no condition to fight this guy. Even if we were fresh as a bunch of daisies, he is an enemy beyond our abilities.

And yet, even now, Moxie grabs her hammer with one hand, her shield with the other, and stands to face this new foe. Pan twirls her bo staff into a ready position. TickTock pulls a small knife from his gizmo belt.

These guys are the best. Don't get me wrong, we're about to die for sure. But I'm proud to die standing next to them. I raise my staff and face the ettin.

Both heads smile. "Such spunk!" says the fancy head. I'm calling this one Steve. "I'm so looking forward to this!"

"Sweet," says the Tim head. "Let's do this."

Moxie limps forward with her hammer raised. Tim and Steve winds up and swings, smashing her right in

Giant mace with notches from all the taters it has stolen.

the chest plate. Moxie flies against the far wall. She does not get up.

"How vexing!" says the Steve head. "Please tell me this isn't going to be over so quickly. I was just starting to enjoy myself!"

Pan pulls out her blowgun and shoots a dart into one of the ettin necks. Nothing happens.

FFFTTT! FFFTTT! FFFTTT!

She pops three more darts into the guy. Nothing.

"Cut it out!" says Tim-head, flicking the darts away. "That tickles!"

Pan shrugs and leaps at the ettin, a cyclone of energy. Her arms swing and her fists fly too fast to see. She makes contact . . . in the gut, in the leg, in the side. You can tell she's hurting him, but it's not enough. It's like a hornet trying to sting a bear to death.

He grabs her by the neck with one hand and round-house punches her with the other.

Pan crashes into the wall near Moxie.

I run to her side. She's conscious, but barely. Moxie has a huge dent in her chest armor. I don't see her breathing.

"Go ahead!" cries Tim-head. "Say goodbye to your friends. Because you're next."

Pan tries to stand, but I put my hand on her shoulder. "Stay down."

My friends are going to die if I don't do something. Something actually heroic. Something actually brilliant. But what? My little dagger is no match for this monster. My feeble spells are worthless at this point.

I feel it again. The paralyzing tightness reminding me how very small, how very average I am. But I grit my teeth and push it away. I pull out my tiny dagger.

If I'm going to die, I'm going to do it defending my friends. That's what heroes do.

And there's nothing average about that.

I step bravely toward the monster . . . and I stumble on the hem of my robes and almost fall into the fire. Dang it! Tim and Steve won't have to kill me. My own robes are going to do it first.

These robes of Master Elmore's have always been too long for me. I look down at them. I look at the firepit I almost fell into. And then it hits me. The one thing I can do.

I turn back to TickTock. "Run," I whisper.

"What?" he asks. "And leave . . . friends?"

"Go hide," I tell him. "Trust me."

He looks uncertainly at me.

"And TickTock," I whisper. "If I don't find you in the next fifteen minutes or so, you should go back to Kevin and tell him we didn't make it."

TickTock gulps. His orange eyes blink back tears. Then he turns and runs out the door.

I hear his feet flapping down the stairs, and he's gone.

The Tim head laughs a deep belly laugh.

"Oh, dreadful luck, old chap!" says Steve-head. "Aban-doned by your little amphibious companion!"

I take one last look at my friends. Pan lets out a little moan. Moxie's face is gray.

I sheathe my dagger. I grit my teeth. And I turn to face the ettin.

The ettin steps forward. He grips his mace with both hands.

I crack my neck. I grab a nearby torch with one hand and hoist up Master Elmore's robes with the other. And then I make my move.

I turn and run like a terrified antelope.

"Hey!" I hear the Tim head yelling behind me. "Get back here!"

I get out of breath easily. So a plan that hinges on my running skills is not a great plan. But I hope it's enough.

I leap up the stairs. Tim/Steve is thundering right behind me. For such a huge creature, he's pretty fast.

When I see the passageway open up on the left, I turn and speed down the slick, sloping path. The ettin is right on me. I can hear his panting breath in my ear.

I'm almost there. The pool lies before me, cold in my torchlight. Gems sparkle brilliantly on the floor ahead. The ground is slick under my feet.

I release my robes. The extra fabric at the bottom immediately gets tangled up in my racing feet, and I stumble headlong to the floor. But this time, it's on purpose.

Tim/Steve is barreling down on me, too close. When I fall, he trips on me hard. The ettin smashes to the ground and slides on the slime-slick floor all the way to the edge of the pool.

He rolls over. "You little jerk!" says the Tim head. "You gave me a boo-boo on my knee!"

"You're going to pay for that!" cries the Steve head.

He reaches for his mace, which lies abandoned at my feet. And that's when it drops.

The rotting ooze.

The ettin's screams tell me that the ooze's acid is already flowing. Even now, it has begun to devour and digest him.

I shudder.

SUPERHEROIC ACHIEVEMENT!
Defeat a Dungeon Boss!
(1,000 Experience Points Awarded)

I feel something on my shoulder and I practically jump out of my skin.

But it's just TickTock. "Fart-boy did tripping on purpose?"

I smile and release a sigh of relief. "Yep. Sure did."

He grins and helps me to my feet. "We go check on Hammer-girl and elf-girl."

I start to follow. But I stop. And bend down.

"Not without this," I say. I grab the ettin's mace. So many notches. So many taters.

"After all, there's a reward," I say triumphantly. "This is proof that we actually defeated the ettin."

I follow the phibling back up the corridor. TickTock looks down at my feet. "Those robes are not fitting you."

"I know. They were my master's robes. I thought I could try and make them fit me."

He shakes his head. "Fart-boy don't need to fit into master's robes. Fart-boy is his own master. Fart-boy needs robes of his own."

I smile. TickTock is totally right.

CHAPTER TWENTY-FIVE

Moxie is dead.

That's all I can think as I rush into the big cavern.

She's still lying on the ground, a big dent in her chest plate. She's bruised and beaten up.

But her eyes are open. And she smiles when she sees me.

Pan is working some of her all-natural healing muck into Moxie's cuts and scrapes.

I tell them about Tim and Steve and the terrible ooze encounter.

"Do you know what this means?" Moxie finally says. The gleam in her eyes says she's back in business mode. "We've beaten the big boss!"

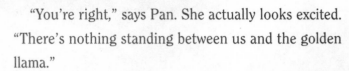

"You're right," says Pan. She actually looks excited. "There's nothing standing between us and the golden llama."

"Why, then, are we standing still?" asks TickTock brightly. "We need to be getting llama toot and making our goodbyes before the other ogres come back!"

It's like we're all sharing a brain.

With Moxie on her feet, we move through the enormous double doors that lie ahead of us.

We enter a cozy chamber.

This is clearly not a golden llama pen.

"Check this out," says Pan, combing through the bric-a-brac on the desk.

"It's a llama!" I cry. "Or at least a carving of a llama."

"Looks like a deer to me," says Pan.

"What do you think it is?" I ask TickTock, showing him the carving. "Llama or deer?"

"That is being a key," says the phibling. "See the notches on the wooden peg? Fits into a lock. TickTock knows locks."

"I bet it's the key to the llama room!" I say. "Since it's shaped like a llama!"

"Deer," mutters Pan.

"We're almost there!" cheers Moxie.

I look around the room for an exit. "But where is it?" I pull aside the tapestry. I look behind the door we came in. Nothing. "We've gone down every corridor. We've opened every door. There's nowhere left to go."

And then it hits me. "Maybe there's a secret door!"

Moxie climbs under the bed.

TickTock gropes the ceiling. I pull the desk from the wall, but I can't see behind it. "Hand me that torch," I tell Pan.

She grabs the torch. But when she pulls it away, the bracket yanks downward with a grinding sound. A lever!

A piece of the wall shudders and moves. A large stone slides into the ground, revealing a long, spiraling staircase going straight down.

We creep down the winding stairs.

They dead-end in a little square foyer. The floor is tiled in gold-and-silver mosaic tiles. A torch burns in another bracket. But that's not all.

On the wall, directly in front of us, are some very strange fancy-pants carvings. We crowd around to take a closer look. And that's when we hear the grinding sound.

We turn. Our staircase is disappearing behind a large stone slab.

We are trapped.

CHAPTER TWENTY-SIX

Panic consumes me. I claw at the stone. "We're trapped! We're trapped!"

TickTock smacks me across the face. "No freaking out, Fart-boy!" he says. "Staying calm. This is just a lock chamber. You open fancy lock, everything opens again. Look!" He points to the carvings on the wall.

Turns out, it's not just a fancy-pants carving on the wall. It's a fancy-pants lock.

"So, how do we open the lock?" I ask TickTock.

He shrugs.

"It's a puzzle lock," says Pan.

"Look." She pulls out the llama/deer stone and

slides the peg into the empty hole on the end. It fits perfectly.

"This is the missing piece," says the elf, winding one of her hair-wispies around a finger. "All of these little carvings are individual pieces with pegs, just like the deer one. We put the pieces in the right order and it opens."

TickTock is super impressed. "Ooh! Elf-girl is good! Nice brain!"

Moxie rubs her hand over the piece in the center. "There's that weird golden snake lady again. Just like at the entrance to the caves. Remember?"

She's right. "It must be important."

"Yeah." Moxie scratches her head thoughtfully. "I totally feel like I've seen that picture before. It's driving me nuts!"

Pan wiggles the pieces in their slots. "Interesting. All the pieces come out except the snake-lady creature. That must mean it's already in the right spot."

"What about this?" Moxie pulls out the pieces. "The snake-lady symbol is the first thing we saw when we came into the dungeon. That's why it goes on top!"

"And the llama is what we're after, right?" I add. "It's the end of the dungeon! So it goes into the bottom slot. Proving that it's not a deer!" I slide the llama piece into place.

"Ooh!" TickTock jumps up and down excitedly. "We are being the warriors! We come into the dungeon . . ." He slides the warrior piece into the second slot.

"The bear could represent the ogres," Pan says. "Remember how Bucket was wearing a bearskin?" Pan slides the bear piece into the slot just above the llama. "The ogres guard the llama."

"Which means the cherry goes in the middle," I say. I reach out to slide it in. Pan darts out to grab my hand.

"Why?" asks Pan.

"Because it's the only slot left!" I shove the piece into place.

"What do you think happens if we get it wrong?" asks Moxie.

There's a grinding noise. "See?" I say proudly. "The door is opening!"

But it's not. There's movement under my heels. I look down. The floor below me is sliding away. TickTock springs onto the wall just in time. I feel myself teetering on the edge. I start to fall.

A hand grabs a fistful of my robes just in time. Pan heaves me back from the open space and onto solid stone.

I look behind me. A deep pit gapes where I'd been standing. Far below, hundreds of spikes wait to impale us.

"MORE SPIKES!" squeaks the phibling. "More spikes is what happens if we get it wrong!"

Both sides of our shiny tiled floor are gone. We are crowded together like flies on a sinking crouton in the middle of a boiling sea of tomato soup.

Trust me. It never works out for the crouton.

My guess is that we have one more chance at this before we're all out of floor.

Pan traces the wall with her hand. "The slots are all set into the links of a chain. Quick, what are some different kinds of chains?"

"Um . . ." I wrack my brain. "Anchor chain?"

"Key chain?" suggests TickTock.

"Chain-mail armor?" says Moxie.

"No . . . no . . . no . . ." Pan starts pacing. "We're thinking too literally."

Moxie shakes her head. "What do you mean?"

"Other kinds of chains," says Pan. "Not actual chains. Think of phrases that have the word chain in them."

I wad my robes in my hands anxiously. "Like . . . chain of command?"

"Yes!" Pan's eyes light up in the torchlight. "What else?"

"Daisy chain!" says Moxie.

"Chain reaction," I suggest.

"Food chain!" Moxie shouts.

"THAT'S IT!" Pan turns back to the puzzle, fingers rapidly tapping against themselves. She grabs all the pieces and lays them out on the floor.

"Look," she says. "What do berries eat?"

I roll my eyes. "Silly elf. Berries are plants. Plants don't eat anything."

"Don't be too sure," says Moxie, pulling her big book out of her backpack. "Buzzlock's book has a carnivorous tree stump called a thorn-gasher that will totally eat you if—"

"Focus, people!" cries Pan. "Berries don't eat anything, so they go at the bottom of the food chain. This," she says, holding the llama/deer piece up, "is a deer."

I look nervously at the spikes gleaming below me. "Fine," I concede.

"What do deer eat?" asks Pan.

"Like, rocks and stuff?" suggests Moxie.

"Plants," says TickTock. "A deer does eating of grass and fruit and berries."

"Exactly!" On the ground, Pan puts the deer piece above the berry piece. "Now, who eats the deer?"

I raise my hand. "I know this one! The bear! The bear eats the deer."

"Yes," says Pan, moving the bear piece over the deer. "And who eats the bear?"

"I do!" says Moxie, rubbing her belly. "Oh man, that's one thing I really miss about Krakentop Academy. Every Thursday night, it was bear stew surprise for dinner."

I reach down and move the warrior piece above the bear. "So, the warrior eats the bear?"

"I think it's maybe just a person," says Pan. "A human or elf or dwarf or whatever."

"Not a phibling," says TickTock. "Phiblings always get left out."

Pan corrects herself. "A humanoid then. An adventurer. A person. Like us!"

"So," I say, squinting down in the torchlight. "Who eats the person? Who eats us?"

All four of our heads move up in unison. All eyes focus on the biggest link. On the top of the chain. On the snake lady.

"That thing," says Pan. "Whatever it is."

A shiver runs up my spine. I turn to Pan. "You sure about this?"

"I am eighty-five percent certain that this is right."

Moxie nods. TickTock nods. Pan looks at me. "We decide together," she says.

"Okay," I say, bracing myself. "Do it."

Pan slides the berry piece into the lowest slot. She slots the deer piece next. Then the bear.

She grips the humanoid piece. "Last one," she says. Her hands quiver.

I reach out to steady the piece in Pan's hand. Tick-Tock touches the bottom. Moxie grabs on from the other side. She's grinning, but it's a nervous grin. "Together," she says.

Together, we slide the last piece in.

The silence is deafening. And then it is replaced by the ominous grind of stone on stone. The floor to our right and left slides back into place. The wall to the

spiral staircase slides open once again. The carvings on the snake-lady piece glow a bright golden light.

The shape of a doorway forms in the stone before us, framing the pieces. The stone archway lowers into the ground, revealing a large open entranceway into a torchlit chamber ahead. The snake-lady piece glows above it.

"You did it, Pan!" I cheer.

"We accomplished it together," she says, nodding appreciatively.

Moxie smacks her palm against her forehead. She points to the glowing piece. "NOW I remember where I've seen that thing!" She's still holding Buzzlock's book in her hands. She flips it open and thumbs her way to the *L*s.

She holds the page open for us to see. "Look! The

picture looks just like that snake-lady thing!" She reads it to us.

A chill zigzags through me. "Oh no," I whisper. "Remember how the word 'llama' was kind of hard to read in Kevin's journal?"

"It barely looked like the word 'llama,'" says Moxie. "That dude has terrible handwriting."

"It's because that's not what he wrote."

"What do you mean?" asks Pan cautiously.

"You were right," I say, turning to Pan. "That puzzle piece wasn't a llama."

From the flickering chamber before us, I hear a soft rustling sound. Like the sound of a baby rattle. Or the tail . . . of a deadly snake . . . right before it strikes.

"There is no golden llama." I gulp the gulp of the seriously horrified. "It's a golden *lamia*."

LAMIA

Can charm a person with the sound of her voice, causing that person to obey any commands. She can use this ability but once per day.

A creature of great evil, half woman, half enormous snake.

The human half can use weapons like swords and bows.

Eats humanoids of all kinds but finds humans particularly delicious.

CHAPTER TWENTY-SEVEN

"What sweet things to write about little old me," comes a slippery voice. "I'm going to have to send that Buzz-lock a thank-you note."

There are two columns just inside the chamber, blocking our view. But in the torchlight we see a snakelike shadow move from within.

"Please, come in."

I turn to stare at the corridor behind us. The way out. We could still make a run for it. I turn to Moxie and Pan. They're thinking the same thing. But Moxie has a cold resolve in her eyes. "We've come all this way," she mutters. "Might as well see it through to the end."

I gulp. End is right.

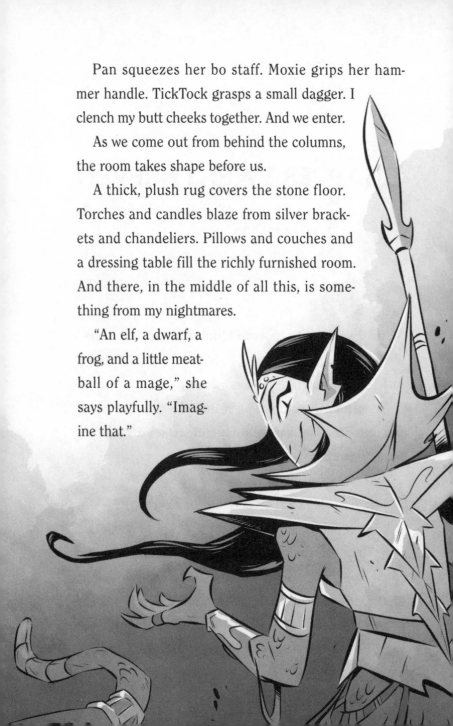

Pan squeezes her bo staff. Moxie grips her hammer handle. TickTock grasps a small dagger. I clench my butt cheeks together. And we enter.

As we come out from behind the columns, the room takes shape before us.

A thick, plush rug covers the stone floor. Torches and candles blaze from silver brackets and chandeliers. Pillows and couches and a dressing table fill the richly furnished room. And there, in the middle of all this, is something from my nightmares.

"An elf, a dwarf, a frog, and a little meatball of a mage," she says playfully. "Imagine that."

Meatball? Really?

For once, TickTock is too scared to protest being called a frog.

"I assume from your presence here that my ogres and my ettin are dead?" the lamia hisses.

"Dang right," says Moxie coldly.

"Such a pity," she croons. "Minions take forever to whip into submission."

"Don't worry," says Moxie. She clenches and unclenches her hammer. "You won't have to train any new minions after we kick your snaky booty."

The lamia slithers toward a nearby couch and relaxes lazily upon it. "Still," she says, "you avoided the Goldenmouth Portal. That is impressive. It's been a long time since that has happened."

"You better believe we avoided it," says Moxie. She leans over to me. "What's the Goldenmouth Portal?"

"I think it's the snake-head trap at the beginning of the dungeon," I mutter.

"Quite right, dear." The lamia's tail flicks casually back and forth. "Tell me, how did you do it?"

"Logic," says Pan simply.

"Interesting." The lamia continues to turn the slender spear in her fingers. "Something lacking in most heroes." She's made no move to attack us. She's just toying with us, like a snake hypnotizing a mouse. Right before she gobbles it whole.

"It's about time those farmers found some heroes with a little bit of brain," she says. "Young though you are, you've done better than most. Still . . . as long as we keep taking their precious taters, they'll keep sending up heroes. It's the most wonderful little delivery service."

"Oh my gosh." Realization hits me. "I wondered why the ogres were taking the taters instead of just eating the farmers. You eat the farmers, the village is gone. You take their taters, and the villagers send you an endless stream of heroes to munch on."

Her lips curl into a smile. "Well done, dear. I've been fattening up that last batch and getting so dreadfully hungry. I thought I would need to eat one soon. But then you stroll in on a silver platter and dinner is served. How thoughtful."

She uncoils from the couch and moves to the center of the room. Her gaze pierces us each in turn. And then she settles on Pan.

"The quiet ones are always the most dangerous," she

croons. Her voice takes on a musical quality. "Come to me, elf child."

"Pan!" Moxie reaches out to grab her. But Pan just shakes her off. "Pan! What are you doing?"

"Not too quick, are you, dear?" the lamia says to Moxie.

"Come closer!" Moxie bellows. "I'll show you how quick I am!" But she's lost some of her bluster.

I grab Moxie to hold her from charging forward. "She's charmed her, Moxie."

Moxie looks confused. "What?"

"Remember in Buzzlock's book? She can charm people." I lower my voice to a whisper. "But only once per day."

Something in Moxie snaps. She pushes past me and bursts toward the snake lady, hammer raised high.

"Defend me, child," says the lamia softly.

Like lightning, Pan moves between Moxie and the lamia.

Her staff is a blur. Before Moxie even realizes what has happened, her hammer flies from her grasp, slamming into one of the columns behind us. Pan coils herself into a ball of energy and punches Moxie with an open palm, square in the chest.

Moxie flies backward, landing at my feet.

TickTock helps me pull Moxie up. Pan has resumed her slow walk toward the lamia. I can see the excitement, the hunger, in the lamia's golden eyes. She's going to chow down on Pan right here and now, with us just watching. And Pan won't be able to do a thing about it.

I turn Moxie around and reach into her backpack. I grope inside until I find it . . . the harpy box. I unlock it with the feather and remove the Bean Burrito of Destiny and the Gas Trapper™.

TickTock reaches out to me. "TickTock don't think that monster gonna eat the Bean Burrito of Destiny. She looks like she wanna eat elf-girl!"

"Yeah," I nod, handing the burrito to TickTock. "I think you're right."

Moxie grabs me. "Then what are you doing?"

"I don't know!" I say. "Something! I'm not going to stand here . . . helpless . . . while Pan gets gobbled up."

I tuck the bottle into my robes and step forward. "Take me instead!"

This gets the lamia's attention. She's almost got

Pan in her grasp, but she stops. Her eyes slither across to me.

"What did you say, boy?"

"Eat me instead!"

"Fart!" I can hear Moxie struggling to charge forward again. But she knows it as much as I do . . . There's no fighting our way out of this one.

"TickTock, you keep her back!" I return my attention to the lamia. "Wouldn't you rather have a nice, healthy human than a twiggy little elf?" I say. "Her little bird bones will probably just get stuck in your throat. Look at her! She's got no meat on her at all."

"Hmm . . ." The creature eyeballs Pan. "She does make rather a skimpy portion." She turns back to me. I can see her looking me over. "Well, bother. I should have charmed the plump one. I see that now."

Plump?

You know what? I am plump. It's about time I embrace my curves.

"You better believe I'm plump," I say. "And probably super delicious. I won't put up a fight." I pull out my silver dagger and drop it to the ground.

"Fart! No!" I hear Moxie choking on her words behind me.

I stay focused. "You just release the elf from your spell and let my friends walk out of here and you've got yourself an all-you-can-eat mage buffet."

She considers for a minute. Her golden eyes hold mine in their gaze. Then . . . "It's a deal. I'll probably even have leftovers." She turns to Pan. "Return to your dwarf friend."

Pan walks back toward us. She and I lock eyes for a moment, and I can see that it's Pan again. The charm has been lifted. A single tear runs down her cheek. I let her pass me, and then I move slowly toward the lamia.

As I approach, the lamia coils her enormous tail around me. First my legs. Then my arms. Then my whole body is encased in the glistening golden scales. I just let it happen.

She leans in close. "Worth mentioning," she whispers. "You're going to make a very generous appetizer. But your dwarf friend is going to be the main course. And the elf will be dessert."

I clench my jaw. "You said you'd let them go."

"I'll let the frog go," she says with a smile. "I'm afraid seafood doesn't agree with me."

CHAPTER TWENTY-EIGHT

I can feel the lamia's scaly coils touching my skin, holding me in place. She's not crushing me. But I'm not going anywhere.

"I don't suppose you'd give the phibling one of your farts before he goes?" I ask her. "Any chance of that?"

She looks taken aback. "One of my . . . farts?"

"It's a long story," I assure her. "He needs it for a science project."

She looks back over at Moxie, Pan, and TickTock.

Her eyes return to me. "I'm going to be so stuffed after I devour the three of you, I imagine I'll have intestinal distress for a week," she says. "So yes, you pathetic child. If your little frog friend wants to wait around, he can have all the gas he wants."

I shake my head calmly. "Well, now you're just embarrassing yourself."

Her eye twitches. "What did you say?"

I hold her golden gaze with a steely one of my own. "He's not a frog, you ignoramus. He's a phibling."

Her face contorts in rage. But then her wide grin returns. I close my eyes as she unhinges her jaw to swallow me whole.

And I say the word.

"Flatulencia."

POOOOF!

The pressure on my body releases as the lamia disappears into a cloud of gas. In seconds, I have the Gas Trapper™ in my hands. I hold it up into the air and press the button, praying that TickTock's little gizmo does its job.

It does.

I pop the cork on and hold it up to Moxie, Pan, and TickTock.

"I find bottled lamia farts are even better than fresh ones," I say with a smile.

SUPERHEROIC ACHIEVEMENT!
Defeat a Super-Powerful
Dungeon Boss!
(1,500 Experience Points Awarded)

Moxie's mouth hangs open. Pan drops her bo staff. TickTock has turned more periwinkle than blue. My friends are so still, I start to worry they were charmed when I wasn't looking. But then Moxie's face explodes into a huge smile.

"FART!" she screams. She rushes at me and crushes me in an enormous bear hug. I've been wrapped in the coils of a lamia, and I can tell you . . . Moxie's hug is stronger.

Pan walks solemnly up to me. "You could have picked Magic Missile as your first spell."

"Here we go again," I say, sighing tiredly.

"You could have picked Sleep!" she exclaims. "Or Blinding Sparkle."

"Yeah, yeah." These little sermons are really starting to wear me down.

Pan places her hands on my shoulders. "But if you had . . . I would be dead."

"Hey!" cries Moxie. "That's true!"

She pulls me into a hug. Which is super awkward. But also kinda nice.

She whispers, "Thank you, my friend. I will never doubt you again."

"Are you okay?" I ask Pan.

"Yes," she says in a hushed voice. "Being completely out of control like that was terrifying."

"I get that," I say. "But hey. Even the elements sometimes lose control."

She smiles softly in surprise. "Do they now?"

"Yep," I nod. "Sometimes the wind has to howl. Sometimes the storm has to rage."

"That's a chaotic thought," she says.

"Yep," I agree. "But also a powerful one."

"Interesting," she says.

TickTock is doing a hoppy little dance. "See? I told you!" he cries. "Even baby heroes are still heroes!"

Moxie retrieves her war hammer. "But this is the whole lamia," she says. "Kevin only wanted the gas."

TickTock takes the bottle from me and holds it up. "A fart is being in there somewhere. Inside the lamia. Let the Great and Powerful Kevin be getting it out himself!" he says.

Pan nods happily. "Agreed."

"I like the way you're thinking, TickTock." I grab the bottle and wrap it carefully back into Moxie's backpack.

Moxie overturns the couch. She lifts up the rug. She rummages through the dressing table.

"What are you doing?" asks Pan.

Moxie huffs in frustration. "Looking for the treasure!" she cries. "This dungeon stinks when it comes to treasure!"

"Over here," says TickTock, padding over to the far end of the chamber.

The phibling examines the far wall, feeling the cracks in the stone with his nimble fingers. Then he reaches up and grabs a nearby torch bracket. An arched segment of the wall lowers into the earth, revealing a dark chamber beyond.

Another spooky, dark, monster-filled chamber? That familiar tightness starts to creep into my chest. But as I look at my friends, I realize: We are together. And we're ready for whatever might be lurking in there. We each grab a nearby torch and slowly enter the darkness.

Cobwebs claw at our faces, burning away at the touch of flames. And then we see it. On the floor to the right . . . something glitters from the shadows.

"Now THAT's what I'm talking about!" says Moxie. She drops her battered shield and picks up the new one, caressing it gently.

From the shadows to my left, I hear a scrabbling. A fluttering. The *scritch-scratch* of legs. My heart starts pounding. I get ready to cast Cozy Camp right into the face of whatever creepy-crawly is coming at us.

My torchlight fills the shadows, illuminating the source of the sound. And I see ...

BIZZY!

Noodle arms or not, I grab Moxie's hammer from her and swing it hard at the padlock, breaking it free. I rush into the cage and am met with an onslaught of slobber and bee drool.

"Look at that," says Pan, pointing to the top of her cage. A mysterious portal glows from the ceiling.

"That snake head at the beginning of the caves must be a magical portal," says Pan. "Anyone or anything that enters it is instantly transported through this opening into these cages."

"For the lamia to eat," mutters Moxie.

Sure enough, the bone that Moxie threw into the opening is right there in the cage with Bizzy. Then, from the far corners of the chamber, I hear more rustling sounds. And . . . voices.

"Get us outta here, man!"

"Hurry! She could come back any time!"

"I'm so scared! Please help us!"

TickTock holds up his torch to illuminate the rest of the chamber. And a great joy fills my heart.

Because there they are. Trapped in four nearby cages.

Giles.

Gridon.

Gorgothar.

And Chico.

It's the Man-Bun Brotherhood. Begging us to rescue them.

Oh, yeah. This day just keeps getting better and better.

CHAPTER TWENTY-NINE

Our treasure haul from the lamia's chamber:

547 gold pieces

14 nice-size gems

Moxie's shiny new shield

Three gorgeous jeweled daggers

And a few other random weapons and pieces of armor that we leave behind

All in all, not a bad bit of loot.

Plus, we found Bizzy alive and well. Priceless.

And the Man-Bun Brotherhood . . . what did they call us when we first met? Feeble runts? Diapered infants? Well, the look on their faces when we rescued them was worth all the gold in the world.

We got out of the Caves of Catastrophe with no problem. I hope that

Bucket doesn't get into too much trouble. Once the ogres return and find Tim and Steve dead, they'll probably wander up into the mountains and cause trouble somewhere else. Maybe Bucket can find a nice little performing group and do dinner theater. I hate to see his talent wasted.

Once out of the caves, Moxie has a brainwave. We get the old, abandoned farmer's cart from near the cave entrance and hook Bizzy up to it like the world's most adorable horse.

And so, only an hour later, we ride back into Taterhaven.

When the villagers see us approaching, they drop their brooms and rakes and come rushing to us.

Chico stands up in the cart to face the cheering crowd.

"Greetings and salutations, fair peasants," he crows. "We, the Man-Bun Brotherhood, have slain the terrible beast that plagues these lands! Furthermore, we have rescued these babes in the woods from the clutches of the beastly monster!"

That no-good, rotten jerk! He's trying to take credit for all of our work!

Gridon, Gorgothar, and Giles step up and join him. They raise their voices in unison.

"For we are the Man-Bun Brotherhood!"

"Giles!"

"Gridon!"

"Gorgothar!"

"And Chico!"

They clearly spend a lot of time practicing. Well, they're not the only ones.

I make the gestures. And I say the words. *"Pepper-puppy-pa-PIE-russ!"*

250

POOF!

Chico . . . is a chihuahua.

Moxie smiles. "Tell the truth," she says to the Man-Bun boys.

"Nay!" shrieks Gorgothar. "See how we are repaid for our heroics! With witchcraft and treachery!"

POOF!

Gorgothar is a poodle.

Pan turns to Gridon. "Tell these people the truth."

Gridon turns to the villagers. "Defend your champions, fair commoners! FOR WE ARE THE MAN-BUN . . ."

POOF!

Gridon is a pug. A really cute one, too.

"Shame!" yells TickTock at Giles. "You tell the truth!"

Giles looks at the puppies standing next to him. He looks at us. He turns to the villagers. And he spills.

"It's true, okay? We didn't defeat the ettin! We didn't destroy the lamia! It was these four!" He points to us and starts bawling. "They rescued us. They're the real heroes. I just want to go home! I miss my mommy!"

I step toward Giles. He flinches at my approach.

"Go on," I say. "Take your puppies and go home."

Giles jumps out of the cart. He grabs all three puppies in his arms and starts running.

"Poor guy," says Moxie. "You turned his buddies into dogs."

"Don't worry," I smile. "I did some reading and it turns out that spell wears off in a couple hours."

"Wait a moment," says Pan with concern. "That means Bizzy's puppy spell ended hours ago."

The four of us turn slowly to the bee. She rushes at us and licks all four of us, buzzing happily.

"Awwwwww!" cries Moxie. "That means she really likes us!"

Taro, the lady from the Yam's Pajamas, steps up to the cart. "Is it true?" she asks. "Did you really destroy Tim and Steve?"

Moxie reaches into the cart and pulls out Tim and Steve's mace. There are hundreds of notches in the handle, representing all the taters he had stolen. She hands it to Taro.

"Behold!" cries a villager. "They carry SpudsBane!"

"They really did it!" cries someone else.

The four of us stand proudly together on the cart. Bizzy buzzes happily before us. "No creatures from the Caves of Catastrophe will ever bother you again!" I announce.

The villagers erupt into cheers. They pass around SpudsBane, taking turns raising the mace over their heads in victory.

From our perch on the cart, I see Taro disappear into the Yam's Pajamas. "I have to admit," cries Fennel. "I thought you kids were a bunch of phonies. Just little tykes playing dress up! Boy, was I wrong!"

"Yeah!" cries Russet. "Who are you heroes?"

Everyone goes silent. They all want to hear the names of the heroes that vanquished their tormentors.

The villagers turn to me.

"And this," Moxie says grandly, "is Bartok the Brilliant."

She got it right. I can't believe it.

"No," I hear myself say.

"HOORAY FOR THE INCREDIBLE FART!" cheer the villagers.

The Incredible Fart. I can't help but grin. Someday,

trumpets far and wide will proclaim the glory of the Incredible Fart. Preferably butt trumpets.

I giggle. Can't help it. It's involuntary.

Moxie starts laughing too. "Hooray for the Incredible Fart!" she yells.

I look at Pan, and she is laughing too. Actually for-real ha-ha laughing. "Hooray for the Incredible Fart!" she says between giggles.

Taro emerges from the inn, a large leather sack in her hands. She approaches our cart.

"A reward was promised!" she cries out in a jolly voice. "It is precious to us. But you heroes have earned it!"

She passes the sack up to me. It is heavy. It bulges with the promise of untold riches.

"What is it?" asks Moxie eagerly.

"Diamonds?" asks Pan softly.

"Tools?" asks TickTock hopefully.

"More gold?" asks Moxie.

I pull the sack open and peek inside. A belly laugh erupts from me. I laugh so hard an accidental fart escapes.

"Well?" cries Moxie. "What is it?"

"What do you think it is?" I cry, holding open the sack for all to see.

TATERS!

CHAPTER THIRTY

The return journey to Kevin's Tower is much more comfortable. We take our time.

During one of our breaks, we pull TickTock aside and present him with a sack of gold and one of the jeweled daggers from the lamia stash.

"Your share of the treasure," says Pan.

For
TickTock?

The phibling pushes it back toward us. "No. Tick-Tock is just a helper."

Pan closes his blue fingers around the dagger. "Not just a helper. You earned it."

He sniffles as Moxie and I step up. "We made you something else," says Moxie. She holds out a little card.

TICKTOCK

Vice-President of Making Cool Gadgets and Being Super Sneaky

"TickTock's own business card!" He starts boo-hooing and doesn't stop until we're back on the road.

We arrive at the tower before dark that same day.

The Great and Powerful Kevin is waiting in the doorway for us.

"Thank goodness," he says. He looks relieved. I'm touched. Maybe he was actually concerned for us after all.

He approaches the phibling. "You goobers didn't break my phibling!" Aw. He cares. In his own weird Kevin way, he cares.

"Not Kevin's phibling," says TickTock knowingly. "Kevin's Vice President of Making Cool Gadgets and Being Super Sneaky!"

"Say what now?" asks Kevin, confused.

"We will do talking later," says the phibling, pointing at us. "Heroes got something for Kevin."

Kevin faces us and rubs his hands together. "So? Did you get it? Did you get the gas of the golden llama?"

"In a manner of speaking," says Pan. She pushes past him into the tower. We follow.

"What do you mean 'in a manner of speaking'?" asks Kevin, chasing us inside.

We lead him into his study behind the curtain. Moxie weaves her way between bubbling beakers and opens the journal on the middle of his table. She flips to the right page and shoves the book at Kevin. "What does that say?" she asks, pointing.

Kevin glances at the writing. "Llama," he says. "Golden llama." He looks at each of us. "What?"

"Read it again," I say.

Kevin reaches into a pocket and pulls out a pair of small spectacles. He hooks them onto his ears and squints through them at the page.

"La......mi......a," he mumbles. He looks up. "Lamia." He grins sheepishly. "Oopsy."

"Oopsy?" cries Moxie.

"Gosh, I wish I could have seen your faces," he says. "That must have been a bit of a shock."

"You think?" I wail. "You sent us in there to face a lamia! THERE'S A BIG DIFFERENCE BETWEEN A LAMIA AND A LLAMA!"

Kevin snaps the book shut and yanks the glasses from his face. "Boo-hoo! Cry me a river," he says. "Would you have taken the quest if you had known you'd be facing a lamia?"

"Maybe not," says Moxie.

"Probably not," says Pan.

"Definitely not!" I cry.

"See?" says Kevin. "I gave you dorks a chance to put your skills to the test. And you passed! You should thank me!"

"Thank you?" I'm amazed.

"You're welcome!" he says with a cocky smile. "So, did you get my lamia gas, or what?"

"Heroes did even better than that," says TickTock.

Moxie removes the bottle from her backpack and holds it before Kevin. "We brought you the whole lamia."

He takes the bottle gingerly.

I grin. "I'm sure she's got a toot in there somewhere for you. If not, just feed her this." I toss him the Bean Burrito of Destiny.

Kevin is silent. I suddenly realize that this might not have been the best plan. It's never a good idea to tick off somebody who has the word 'powerful' in their name.

Then he snorts out a laugh. "That'll work, you weirdos," he says. "TickTock and I can take precautions before we unbottle her."

He crosses the room and lifts the lid on an enormous chest. "I'm sure you got some sweet loot during your little adventure," he drawls. "Still. I promised to make it worth your while."

He rummages around inside. He pulls out a pair of strappy sandals.

"For the monk," he says, holding out the shoes. "Sassy Sandals of Silence."

Pan receives them reverently. "What do they do?" she asks.

"They make your footsteps completely silent," says Kevin. "You could run through a whole field of cheese doodles in those and not make a peep."

Pan bows gratefully.

"For the warrior . . ." Kevin reaches into the chest. "How about a magical axe?"

Moxie turns her gaze upon Master Redmane's war hammer. "No thanks," she says. "I'm kind of attached to this."

"Suit yourself," Kevin says, dropping the axe back into the chest with a clatter. He looks thoughtfully at Moxie. He snaps his fingers. "I got the perfect thing for you."

He reaches into a nearby drawer and pulls out a little silk pouch. It rattles as he shakes it tauntingly at Moxie.

"It's called a Bag of Bones," says Kevin. "It contains four little carved animal figurines. When you reach in and throw one to the floor, it becomes a full-grown version of that animal. It will fight to the death for you! Or until that fight is over. In that case, it'll just disappear."

Moxie claps her hands together. "How cool! What animals are they?"

Kevin grins. "No idea. That's the fun part! You don't know until you pull one out." He tosses the pouch to her.

He looks over at me. "And for the little magic man."

264

Kevin reaches into the chest and pulls out several rolls of parchment.

"Three magic scrolls. One will cast Squiddly Diddly. One will cast Stone to String Cheese. And the last one will cast Barlowe's Belching Bubble."

My mouth is hanging open. "I've heard of those spells. They're very advanced. I can't cast any of those yet."

Kevin rolls his eyes. "Scrolls are different, doofus. Your level doesn't matter."

"What?" I ask. "How?"

"It's not like your spellbook. With a scroll, the magic is embedded in the paper. You just read them right off the scroll. But bear in mind . . . scrolls are one-time use. They burn up as soon as you use them. So pick your moment."

I take them carefully in my hands. Wow. I feel drunk with power.

And then I hear it. Clapping.

I look up. The Great and Powerful Kevin . . . is applauding us. And he's not even being sarcastic. I can see from the look on his face. This powerful mage is truly impressed.

I guess this is what glory and honor feel like. I could get used to this.

"So?" Kevin closes the chest and looks us over. "What's next for you dweebs?"

We look at one another. We're not sure. We've been so focused on surviving that we never planned what would come next.

Kevin spots our indecision. "Tell you what," he says. "You did good on this quest. I'm not gonna lie, I didn't expect you to pull though. Surviving against ogres. And a lamia! That's no small potatoes."

I beam under this praise. I'm not sure if heroes are supposed to beam. But I can't help myself.

"Why don't you head to Conklin?" Kevin suggests. "There's a place there called the Woozy Wyvern Inn. It's a good place to chill out for a while. TickTock and I might have some more work for you later, if you're interested."

Oh, we're interested. The Great and Powerful Kevin rewards us in magic items, not taters. I'm no expert. But that seems like a step in the right direction.

Conklin it is.

CHAPTER THIRTY-ONE

Conklin is a proper town.

It bustles with travelers, shops, and market stalls.

We rent three rooms for a month at the Woozy Wyvern. With all our lamia gold, we can afford it.

After a couple days of rest, we go out to spend some of our loot. Our masters' hand-me-down gear has served its purpose, but it wasn't made for us. My robes are torn and shredded. Moxie's armor is dented and banged.

We look amazing in our new gear.

After our shopping spree, most of our cash is gone. Being a hero is expensive! We're going to have to find a new quest soon.

PAN SILVERSNOW, ZEN MASTER OF THE ELEMENTS

Sleek embroidered monk robes!

Slick new bo staff! (It's the lamia's spear!)

Fancy and fashionable hair accessories!

BIZZY, GIANT BUMBLEBEE OF CUTENESS

Bizzy's brand-new cart!

Yellow and black trim, to match Bizzy!

But before we do, it's time we properly put some things to rest.

And so, on a crisp morning about a week after arriving in Conklin, we find ourselves on a lonely hill outside of town. We dig three deep holes.

And we say goodbye to our masters once and for all.

There are no bodies to bury. So we take their armor and weapons. The stuff we wore and wielded on our great Fart Quest. We bury these.

We each keep something. Moxie will never let Master Redmane's hammer out of her sight.

Pan wears a simple jade hair clip from Master Oonah.

And I have Master Elmore's spellbook slung

on my shoulder. But I also keep Master Elmore's staff, which leans against a nearby tree. It just seems wrong to bury it.

"Master Redmane found me as an orphan when I was four years old," says Moxie wistfully. "He was like a father to me." She sniffles and wipes her eyes with the back of her hand.

Pan kneels and whispers a soft chant. "Master Oonah was the wisest person I have ever known. I am grateful for what she passed on to me. And I am ready to forge my own path. With power. And maybe a little chaos."

Her hair-wispies fall out of her hair clip, into her face. And, for the first time since I've known her, she just lets them dangle there.

"Pan," I say. "You're not fixing your hair."

"What can I say?"

She shrugs, glancing my way. "Sometime the wind has to howl."

I grin. Then I realize . . . it's my turn. I wrack my brain to think of something nice to say about Master Elmore. "Master Elmore . . . sure was a mage," I say feebly. "And he had the toughest toenails I've ever seen."

It's not enough. I look down at the spellbook hanging from my side. Its pages are thick and wrinkled with years of use. It contains spells I won't be able to use for a long time. But it also contains Gas Attack. Which saved our lives.

I realize something. Master Elmore wasn't always the grumpy old guy that I knew. He was once young, like me. He accomplished great deeds. He earned the name Elmore the Impressive. And he was still willing to take on a goofball apprentice like me.

I clear my throat. "I am honored to have been taught by Elmore the Impressive. I hope that someday I can be as impressive as he was."

Pan looks over at me. "That's lovely, Fart."

A silence falls over us as we stare at the graves.

I reach out and grab Master Elmore's staff. The dark crystal at the top, which has been dull and unshining since Master Elmore's death . . . suddenly pulses with life. But not purple, as it always did for Master Elmore. It glows a yellowish green. Kind of a . . . fart green.

A new color. For a new mage. Me.

Moxie grins. "You look super impressive in those snazzy robes and glowy staff," she says.

"You know what would really be impressive?" asks Pan.

I roll my eyes. "I have a feeling you're about to tell me."

She turns to me and smirks. "If you learned Magic Missile next. It's kind of your duty."

I giggle under my breath. "Heh-heh. You said doody."

Moxie giggles.

I turn to Pan. "Number one . . . you're not the boss of me. And number two . . ." I shape my hands into a star, point them at a nearby tree, and mutter:

Moxie cheers and pumps her fist in the air. "Yeah!" she exclaims. "You've been studying!"

SUPERHEROIC ACHIEVEMENT!
Learn a New Spell!
(500 Experience Points Awarded)

I feel a surge of confidence. And with the casting of this new spell, a new surge of power runs through me.

CONGRATULATIONS!
LEVEL UP!
You are now Level 2!

I turn to Pan. But she's just giggling. She can't stop laughing. I've never seen her like this.

"What is the matter with you?" I ask.

She catches her breath. "You said 'number two.'" She laughs so hard she accidentally squeezes out a fart. Then she dissolves into a fit of uncontrollable snickers.

"P-U, Pan!" cries Moxie. "Elf farts stink!"

"What can I say?" Pan laughs. "Sometimes the storm has to rage!"

We all burst into giggles as we turn and head back to Conklin.

I am the Incredible Fart. I realize I'll never be as impressive as Elmore the Impressive. But that's okay. Because I have something I've never really had before.

Friends. Maybe even a family.

Whatever quest awaits us next, Pan, Moxie, and I will face it together.

The Super-Secret Diary of
THE GREAT AND POWERFUL KEVIN
PRIVATE THOUGHTS! KEEP OUT!
THIS MEANS YOU!

I have the first ingredient in my possession. The gas of a golden lamia.

I figured those three goofy kids I hired wouldn't even make it to Taterhaven. I never imagined they'd actually survive the Caves of Catastrophe.

This is going to work out perfectly. Now that I have the first item to make my artifact of despicable destruction, those three boneheads are going to get all the ingredients on my evil shopping list.

After crushing their very first quest, young adventurers Pan, Moxie, and Fart are hungry for their next challenge. Luckily, the Great and Powerful Kevin has cooked up something for the trio: locate a bedazzler—a rare and monstrous creature of truly horrific power—and bring back . . . its barf.

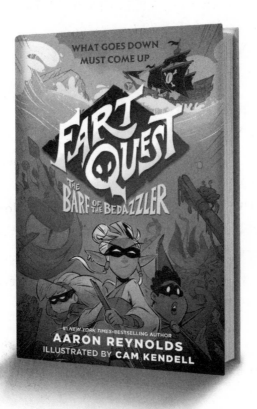

Keep reading for an excerpt.

CHAPTER ONE

We are totally surrounded.

The spindernots are closing in fast. And they out-number us ten to one.

SPINDERNOT

Disgusting.

Invades enchanted woods.

Gobbles up fairies and sprites.

Moxie, Pan, and I stand together. Warrior, monk, and mage. Dwarf, elf, and human. We form a triangle of awesomeness against these spidery foes.

I charge forward, ready to unleash my magic against these foul denizens of the forest. But some freaky unseen force holds me back. I am powerless! WHAT UNSPEAKABLE WITCHCRAFT IS AT WORK HERE?

"FART!" Pan calls to me. "Your robes are caught on that branch."

Oh. Apparently there is no unspeakable witchcraft at work here. Just a grabby tree.

I tug hard. The branch snaps free, sending me face-first into the dirt. I bump against Moxie. Who drops her hammer. Which falls on Pan's toe. Pan yowls in pain.

Dang. I was having such an empowering moment too.

My name is Fart.

Truth is, the three of us are not quite as mighty as I like to imagine. Really, we're just Level 2 heroes. Barely a step above newbie apprentices.

So where does that leave us? Oh, yeah.

We are totally surrounded.

Sensing our weakness, the spindernots have regrouped. Spinning a wall of webs, they slowly close in on us.

Things are not going according to plan, so Moxie does what Moxie does best. Takes action.

She pulls a small pouch from her belt. It's the magical bag of animal statues that she earned at the end of our last quest.

Gosh, I hope it does something cool.

She plucks a small figurine from the pouch and tosses it to the ground. It's a tiny hippo, meticulously carved and super adorable.

POOF! The figurine disappears and a full-size hippopotamus takes its place. The hippo lets out an earsplitting roar and charges the spindernots, sending them skittering for cover.

Yep. It does something cool.

The distraction buys me enough time to get to my feet.

I mentally run through the list of spells that I know:

FART'S SPELL LIST

 Gas Attack—My trademark spell

 Feather Friend—I can talk to birds

 Magic Missile—Shoots a flaming dart

 Puppy Power—Turns baddies into puppies

 Cozy Camp—Creates a small campfire. It's a baby spell, but perfect for the job right now.

"Flimmity-flamesh." A tiny magical fire sparks from my hands, burning away the closest webs.

Pan takes her cue. Using her monk ability to manipulate the elements, she sends the flames skittering across the webs, burning them away but carefully avoiding the trees. The last thing we want to do is torch the enchanted forest we were hired to protect.

We might not get paid. Plus Pan really loves trees.

Moxie's hippo tramples several spindernots and bashes into a tree, sending more spindernots scattering for cover. Moxie chases after it, twirling her hammer like a whirlwind.

KA-BLAMMO!

With one mighty swing, she sends six spindernots flying through the air.

Wow. Moxie's skills are getting impressive.

Pan snuffs out the flames, grabs her bo staff, and pole-vaults over the retreating spindernots. Doing a triple backflip, she lands and blocks their escape with her spinning staff.

Holy cow. I didn't know Pan could even do that.

A little niggle of jealousy rears up in me. Pan and Moxie are becoming super powerful. And I'm still casting my cute little Cozy Camp. I reach into my mind, trying to muster the words to the new spell I've been memorizing. It's time to show my friends that I can be impressive and amazing too.

I concentrate and mutter the magical words *"Plaintanitar au musa!"* Banana peels shoot from my palms. The spindernots slip. They slide.

The spindernots collapse in a heap. Moxie and the hippo leap upon them with abandon.

Dwarf hammer wallops. Hippo feet stomp.

KA-POW! KA-BLAM! KA-BLOOEY!

And, just like that, no more spindernots.

SUPERHEROIC ACHIEVEMENT!
Defeat a Horde of Spindernots!
(250 Experience Points Awarded)

Pan brushes dirt from her robes. "Nice work," she says. "Though I hesitate to point out that an enormous hippo and flying banana peels were not part of our carefully constructed plan."

Moxie shrugs. "What can I say? There were more spindernots than we thought. We had to improvise!"

The elf tucks her stray hair-wispies back into her topknot. "I am not a fan of improvisation."

"Aw, come on," says Moxie, shoving her playfully. "You're no fun."

"Fun?" says Pan. "I admit, fun is not my main priority."

"Speaking of fun improvisation," Moxie says,

shooting me a huge smile, "Cute spell, banana brain! That was hilarious!"

"Cute?" I cry. "Hilarious? Don't you mean impressive? And amazing?" I step toward our conquered foes, slip on a banana peel, and land on my butt.

"Well, that *was* impressive," says Pan with a smirk. "You only fell down twice during that fight."

I flush with embarrassment and chuck a banana

peel at her. She dodges it easily and yanks me to my feet.

With the spindernots vanquished, the magically summoned hippo nuzzles Moxie and disappears with a *POOF!*

Pan surveys the glade. "What a mess."

She's right. It looks like a gang of angry gnomes had a weeklong piñata party in this place.

It's not pretty. But we stand victorious.

And yet danger still lurks. Because we hear the fluttering of insect wings behind us.

We turn, hammer, staff, and spells at the ready.

But it's just our employer.

Ephemera. The pixie.

Want to wield a bo staff like Pan,
swing a hammer like Moxie, or turn someone
into a stinky gas like Fart?

Check out
FART QUEST: THE GAME
to continue the smelly saga with our heroes!

Don't miss the other books in the
FART QUEST series . . .

And coming soon,
Fart Quest: The Troll's Toe Cheese

mackids.com

AARON REYNOLDS is a *New York Times*–bestselling author of many highly acclaimed books for kids, including the Caldecott Honor book *Creepy Carrots!*, *Nerdy Birdy, Dude!*, and *The Incredibly Dead Pets of Rex Dexter*. As a longtime Dungeon Master and lover of Dungeons & Dragons, Aaron is no stranger to epic quests. He lives in the Chicago area with his wife, two kids, four cats, and between zero and ten goldfish, depending on the day. **aaron-reynolds.com**

CAM KENDELL is an illustrator of all things absurd and fantastical; creator of comics such as *Choose Your Gnome Adventure*, *Mortimer B. Radley: The Case of the Missing Monkey Skull*, and *Flopnar the Bunbarian*; and artist for board games like D&D's Dungeon Mayhem: Monster Madness and 5-Minute Mystery. When not drawing gnomes and/or goblins, Cam enjoys birding, rocking on the accordion, losing at board games, and hiking in the beautiful Utah mountains with his wife and four children, hoping to see a black bear … from a safe distance. **camkendell.com**